AKEELAH
AND THE
BEE

A Novel by James W. Ellison

Based on the Screenplay by Doug Atchison

Newmarket Press • New York

This book is published in the United States of America.

First Edition

ISBN-13: 978-1-55704-729-8
ISBN-10: 1-55704-729-4

10 9 8 7 6 5 4 3 2

Library of Congress Cataloging-in-Publication Data
Ellison, James Whitfield.
  Akeelah and the bee : a novel / by James Whitfield Ellison ; based on the screenplay by Doug Atchison. — 1st ed.
      p. cm.
  ISBN-13: 978-1-55704-729-8 (pbk. : alk. paper)
  ISBN-10: 1-55704-729-4 (pbk. : alk. paper)
  I. Atchison, Doug. II. Akeelah and the bee (Motion picture) III. Title.
PZ7.E47648Ake 2006
[Fic]—dc22
                                        2006012760

QUANTITY PURCHASES
Companies, professional groups, clubs, and other organizations may qualify for special terms when ordering quantities of this title. For information or a catalog, write Special Sales Department, Newmarket Press, 18 East 48th Street, New York, NY 10017; call (212) 832-3575; fax (212) 832-3629; or e-mail info@newmarketpress.com.

www.newmarketpress.com

Manufactured in the United States of America.

AKEELAH

AND THE

BEE

The Present

Akeelah Anderson, small and skinny for a just-turned-twelve-year-old and smart beyond her years, sits in her bedroom staring at her image in the mirror and engaging in one of her favorite pastimes: daydreaming. She removes her glasses, cleans them on the sleeve of her blouse, then replaces them in a single, flowing, absent-minded movement. Slowly her image breaks into a smile.

"Akeelah," she says in a surprisingly low voice, given her age and slight physical stature, "what a journey for a girl from South Los Angeles. Girls from this neighborhood just aren't supposed to have journeys like this. Everything seems like a dream. I know this happened and that happened and a whole bunch of other things, too, but it should seem more real than it does. What's the word for what I'm feeling? Come on, girl, words are what you're good at. What is it you're reaching for? 'Verisimilitude'? 'Somnambulism'? 'Déjà vu'? Nope—they're all wrong. But there's gotta be a word for it because it's how I've been feeling all year and it just doesn't go away...."

She sticks out her tongue and crosses her eyes. "You're crazy, girl, plain loco, talking to yourself this way. If you start answering yourself, you'll know you're in big, big trouble.

"Maybe the word I'm searchin' for is...what? Maybe it's 'magic.' Human magic...."

One

The Anderson family—mother, two sons, and two daughters—lived in a mostly black neighborhood in South Los Angeles, a dangerous, forlorn area that often erupted in violence, especially on Saturday nights and most especially on the hot nights of summer. It was light-years removed from the glitter and glamour of Hollywood and the majestic coastline to the west. Akeelah attended Crenshaw Middle School, an unkempt institution with gang graffiti scrawled on the walls. There were dangling pipe fixtures in the bathrooms where, in better times, the sinks used to be. African-American and Hispanic kids crammed into the overflowing classrooms, shouting, cursing, pushing one another, and ignoring the teachers who implored them to quiet down and take their seats. The teachers, for the most part, were tolerated but not obeyed. Already at ten, eleven, and twelve, many of the students at Crenshaw resented any official forms of discipline and fought against them with street anger and street smarts.

Ms. Cross, a petite teacher in her early forties, with lines of worry etched in her features, walked down a row of desks occupied by rowdy seventh-graders. Like all the classes at Crenshaw Middle School, Ms. Cross's was over-crowded. There were nearly forty students jammed into a small space. They all wore school uniforms, and many of the girls were already wearing makeup. Ms. Cross handed out graded spelling tests. She tried to put on a smiling face, but gave up the effort as the noise level increased.

"You're all in the seventh grade now," she said. "What does that mean to you?"

"It mean we be in the eighth grade next year," said a tall boy lounging in the back of the room.

"Not necessarily, Darian," the teacher said. "What it means is, when I give you a list of words, you *study* them. Middle school means taking more responsibility. The average score on this test is very upsetting—barely 50 percent. Totally unacceptable. I know you can do better, but you have to work at it…." She paused in front of Akeelah's desk. Akeelah was busy whispering with her best friend, Georgia.

"Akeelah," Ms. Cross said, "I hate to break into your very private conversation."

She turned to the teacher and said, almost under her breath, "That's sarcasm, ain't it, Ms. Cross?"

She tried to restrain a smile.

"I guess you could say that. Tell me something. How long did you study for this spelling test?"

Akeelah shifted her eyes uneasily to some of her classmates who were following this exchange intently. She knew what lay behind the teacher's question and she didn't like it. In Crenshaw Middle School the wisest course was to remain anonymous, not to stand out, and above all, never to appear smarter than the other students. And even above that, it was important never, ever to be labeled as the teacher's pet.

She said with a shrug, "I didn't study for it."

The teacher looked at her with surprise, an eyebrow lifted. "You didn't?"

"No, ma'am." She looked bored and uninterested, a pose she had developed in the past year as protective covering. Being smart was dangerous. She had learned that lesson the hard way, having accumulated in the past year a collection of bruises and bloody noses.

Ms. Cross slapped the test facedown on her desk.

"See me after class," she said.

Akeelah reached for the test and then pulled her hand away. "Why? I ain't done nothin' wrong."

"There's some things I have to discuss with you."

Akeelah turned to Georgia and giggled. The moment Ms. Cross walked away and the eyes of her classmates were no longer on her, Akeelah casually lifted up a corner of her test. 100 percent. Thirty words and thirty perfect spellings. When Georgia tried to sneak a look, Akeelah covered the test with her hand.

When the bell rang there was a stampede for the door to see who could escape first. Akeelah sat at her desk until the room was completely emptied out and then slowly approached Ms. Cross's desk. Through the small window in the door, Georgia tried to get her attention, but Akeelah ignored her.

The teacher looked up and studied her solemnly. "You're not telling the truth."

Akeelah went into an indignant hip-locked stance. "What do you mean?"

"You did study for the test, didn't you?"

"It don't make no difference if I did or not. It's just...I wish you wouldn't ask me stuff in front of the others."

Ms. Cross regarded her for a moment, slowly nodding her head. "You don't like to call attention to yourself, do you, Akeelah?"

She looked away and pressed her lips together in silence.

"You know," she said, "you could be one of my very best students—probably *the* best. But I keep asking myself, Why aren't you? What's holding you back? You don't turn in half your homework, and sometimes you don't even show up for class. So what's going on?"

Akeelah shrugged. "I don't know."

"I have a feeling you do know."

"Maybe I'm not as smart as you think I am."

"But you are. Does the work bore you?"

"Yeah. It's kind of boring."

"Would you like it if I gave you advanced assignments?"

"I don't know."

She spotted Georgia staring through the window making faces at her and started to giggle.

"Please," Ms. Cross said, clearly frustrated. "Try to pay attention."

Reluctantly Akeelah turned back to her. "Sorry."

The teacher cleared her throat, swiveled a pen around

between her thumb and first finger. Finally she said, "Akeelah—do you know about next week's spelling bee?"

"No."

"It's been posted on the bulletin board for weeks."

"I don't pay no attention to the bulletin board."

"Well, I think you should sign up for it."

She handed her a flyer for Crenshaw's Inaugural Spelling Bee. Akeelah's eyes swept over the flyer, then she let out an annoyed breath.

"I'm not interested."

"But why? You have a real talent for spelling. Some of the words on the test I gave you were very, very difficult—'picnicking,' for instance." She smiled. "I misspelled that in college."

"'Picnicking' wasn't hard, Ms. Cross," she said. "None of the words were really hard."

"Which is why you should be in the spelling bee."

Akeelah gave a barely perceptible shake of her head.

"Can I go now?" she said.

A very disappointed Ms. Cross stared after her as she slung her book bag over her slender shoulder and left the classroom.

*

Akeelah and Georgia, both of whom had seen the movie *Hustle & Flow* the week before, walked home from school singing "It's Hard Out Here for a Pimp," laughing and snapping their fingers. The South Los Angeles neighborhood was grim but they were hardly aware of the boarded-up storefronts, the walls crawling with gang graffiti, the broken windows and sidewalks, and the littered streets. They had grown up in South Los Angeles and it had always been the same. They expected nothing from it, and it gave them nothing in return.

Georgia and Akeelah had been best friends since they were toddlers. Georgia was kind and easy-going, and one secret of their friendship was that Georgia accepted Akeelah for who she was—a really smart girl. She was proud of her friend and Akeelah knew it.

"Devon home on leave, right?" Georgia said when they had exhausted the hip-hop song.

"Yeah," Akeelah said. "He's got a two-week leave."

Devon, her twenty-year-old brother and the pride of the family, was in training to become a pilot. Akeelah had felt sad when he left for the service. With her father gone, Devon was the one significant adult male in her life.

"Your brother fine," Georgia said. "I got it all figured out. One day he gonna be the pilot of a big commercial jet and I'm gonna be the flight attendant."

Akeelah nodded, barely paying attention. Her mind kept returning to her conversation with Ms. Cross. Why was she pushing her so hard? She was a good speller, but why would she put herself in the position of being the school nerd—a freak for others to stick pins in? No way....That was not going to happen.

They passed a weathered-looking man hanging outside a liquor store. He was suffering from the shakes. His skin was the consistency of old leather, full of fine cracks and fissures, and his breathing sounded like steam escaping from a leaky pipe. He had been hanging out on the street as long as Akeelah could remember, and he symbolized for her all that was wrong with South Los Angeles.

"Got any change for an ol' man, girls?"

Akeelah noticed that the whites of his eyes when he gazed at her were not white but the color of egg yolks.

"You wouldn't be so old if you stopped drinkin' that Night Train Express."

He shook his head.

Georgia said, "Leave Steve alone. He's a good ol' guy."

Steve blinked rapidly and grinned. He was missing most of his bottom front teeth.

Georgia giggled as Akeelah kicked a soiled grapefruit half and two Budweiser cans off the sidewalk.

"This neighborhood is *wack*," she said as she reached in her purse and withdrew two quarters and placed them in Steve's outstretched, trembling hand. "Hey, drink yourself stupid, ol' man. Maybe that's the only answer around here."

Georgia shook her head. "Girl, you always trippin'."

As they reached the corner, a new Ford Explorer passed by, a rap song pumping full blast from the stereo. A young black man, Derrick-T, was behind the wheel. He gave the girls a wave and a grin. Derrick-T was famous in the neighborhood for the quick fortune he had amassed dealing drugs. Akeelah disliked him, certain he was a bad influence on her fourteen-year-old brother Terrence, who aped Derrick-T's clothes and mannerisms and took great pride in riding up front with him.

"Dang," Georgia said, "Derrick-T's new ride is *tight*."

"He been tryin' to get Terrence in trouble."

"Come on, Kee. Your bro can get his own self in trouble."

"You just don't like Terrence."

"I like him all right. He's always trippin', just like you. Only in a different way."

They walked for a block in silence until Georgia said, "Okay—aren't you gonna tell me?"

"Tell you what?"

"What did Cross Face want? All that hush-hush stuff."

"Nothin'. Just a whole rap about some stupid spelling bee. She tried to talk me into it, like I'm some freakin' spelling genius."

"Well, you are good, you know," Georgia said quietly. "You gonna do it?"

"Nah."

"You'd probably do really good, Kee. You ace those tests."

"Can you see me gettin' up in front of everybody? I'd pee my pants for sure."

Two

Akeelah's bedroom was an expression of her inner-most self, that secret part of her that she kept hidden from her family, even from her best friend, Georgia. Only the photograph of her dead father shared the room with her and her secret passions. A year ago Akeelah made a pact with her mother: she would dust and vacuum her room and change her bedsheets on Saturday, and in exchange Tanya, her mother—a loving woman but a decided busybody, in Akeelah's opinion—would stay out of her room unless invited in.

Stacks of books, mainly classics and contemporary novels, lined the shelves and were piled up around an ancient computer. A game of computer Scrabble was in progress. Akeelah was hunched over the screen, studying it with a scowl of intense concentration. She muttered under her breath for a moment and then used all her remaining letters to spell "fuchsia," and racked up 69 points. A small smile curved her lips and she whispered, "Way to go, girl."

A moment later her older sister, Kiana, a single moth-er at the age of seventeen, burst into the room.

"You're supposed to knock," Akeelah said, still facing the screen.

"Mama says come eat."

17

Akeelah sighed and turned slowly in her chair. "You're the only one that don't knock, Kiana."

"I guess that makes me different."

"I guess it does. It makes you a pest."

"Mama's not in a good mood. You better get your skinny butt to the table."

Akeelah looked back at the screen wistfully. "I just got my highest score ever."

"Well, whoop-de-doo. Do you think I care? The food's on the table, li'l sister. Shake it."

The Andersons ate their meals in the kitchen and the aroma was always delicious. The rich smell of beef stew made Akeelah's stomach growl. She seldom thought of eating as anything more than a natural function to maintain strength and life, but suddenly she felt famished. Her eating habits were a source of frustration to her mother because no matter how hungry Akeelah might profess to be, a few bites seemed to fill her up.

Devon sat at the head of the table. Tall and handsome, he wore his hair in a military brush cut. From the way his mother looked at him, her eyes aglow, a tender smile on her lips, it was clear that her oldest child was the apple of her eye.

He looked up from his plate and winked at Akeelah.

"And how's my baby sister?"

"I'm fine."

She felt bashful around Devon. He was too good-looking and too charming, she felt, to be a member of the family.

Kiana flounced into a chair and pouted as she began

to feed her baby daughter, who sat in a high chair making gurgling sounds. In the living room the TV was playing at high volume.

"I'm your baby sister, too, Devon," Kiana pointed out.

"So you are," he said. "But you're also a mother. And you've lost your baby fat."

"I've never had any baby fat," Akeelah said.

"Shut up," Kiana said. "Nobody asked you."

"Mama," Devon said, quickly changing the subject, "I've been dreamin' about your cookin' for the past five months. Military chow does not cut it."

"Thank you for those kind words," Tanya said. "Least I got one child who appreciates what I do 'round here." Suddenly she frowned, touching her throat with her hand. "Where's Terrence at? He should have been home from practice an hour ago."

"Three guesses, Ma," Akeelah said.

"Don't get smart, young lady."

"He's probably hangin' with Derrick-T."

"Derrick-T?" Devon said, looking up from his plate. "That boy still alive?"

"Not after you get done with him," Akeelah said, smiling. "I know how you two feel about each other."

"That's right, princess. Bad feelings all the way back to kindergarten. He's got no damn sense and never did. Why does he want to hang out with a kid like Terrence, anyway?"

"Somebody to Step 'n' Fetch for him."

Tanya gave Akeelah a sharp glance. "Watch your mouth."

Devon laughed. "This girl's a smart one, Mama." He reached for Akeelah's hand. "Give me some sugar," he said.

Akeelah leaned forward and kissed him on the cheek.

"Look, Ma," Kiana said. "The girl's blushing."

"So how many planes you shot down so far?" Akeelah said, ignoring her sister.

"So far? Zero. You don't do much shootin' when they got you behind a computer screen in Nevada. Don't make me out to be a war ace—not yet, anyway."

"And that's good, as far as I'm concerned," Tanya said. "We want you on the ground where you belong."

"Devon *looks* like a war ace," Kiana said. "Denzel at the controls."

"He don't look anything like Denzel," Akeelah said.

Devon laughed. Rubbing Tanya's shoulder, he said, "Mama, I'm gonna have my wings and my college degree before you know it." He reached out his other hand and tousled Akeelah's hair. "Unless this one beats me to it. I wouldn't bet against her."

Tanya's mouth tightened. "Not if she keeps skippin' class with Georgia Cavanaugh, she won't. Akeelah—go turn off the TV."

"Ah, Ma, leave it on," Kiana said. "It soothes the baby."

"You mean it soothes you."

Devon whispered in Akeelah's ear, "Flip it over to ESPN real quick. Check out the Lakers score."

Akeelah giggled as she left the table. She walked into

the living room and switched on ESPN. Instead of the Lakers game, she found a telecast of a spelling bee. A thirteen-year-old, red-haired girl was at the mike. She rubbed her hands together nervously, but when she spoke she sounded confident, even slightly arrogant. "...c-e-p-t-o-r," she spelled slowly but with assurance. "'Nociceptor.'"

Akeelah gazed at the screen, open-mouthed. "What's this?" she muttered to herself. She lowered herself onto the couch without moving her eyes from the screen. They had spelling on TV? Did other people really care about this stuff?

"I said turn it off, Akeelah," Tanya shouted from the kitchen.

Akeelah barely heard her mother's words. She watched curiously as the vast audience applauded the girl. Next, a thirteen-year-old Japanese boy named Dylan Watanabe marched up to the mike, a superior smirk on his handsome face.

The Pronouncer gave him his word. "'Brunneous.'"

As the boy hesitated, Akeelah started mouthing the letters. "B-r-u-n..."

Finally the boy began spelling. "B-r-u-n-e-o-u-s. 'Brunneous.'"

A bell sounded and a demoralized Dylan sat down, while the red-haired girl marched up to the mike again.

"Akeelah," Tanya shouted again, now plainly annoyed. "Turn off the television and *come eat*. I mean *now!*"

The red-haired girl again spelled slowly and with confidence. "B-r-u-n-*n*-e-o-u-s. 'Brunneous.'"

"That is correct," the Head Judge said. "If you spell

21

the next word correctly, you will be the new national champion."

Akeelah leaned forward on the couch, her eyes narrowed with curiosity and concentration.

The Pronouncer slowly said, "'Schottische.'"

The red-haired girl could not restrain a smile. "'Schottische,'" she said, her voice firm and clear. "S-c-h-o-t-t-i-s-c-h-e."

"Congratulations!" intoned the Head Judge. "You are the new Scripps National Spelling Bee champion."

Akeelah watched the girl jump for joy as she was handed a huge check for $20,000. She was swarmed by photographers as she waved the check in the air.

"Dang, that's a lot of money," Devon said, popping his head into the living room. "Maybe Akeelah should try out for something like that."

Tanya also poked her head in. "Maybe Akeelah should try listening for a change," she said. "Now turn the set off and come eat."

Akeelah clicked it off reluctantly and returned to the table, but she had heard nothing that either her brother or her mother had said. Her mind was a million miles away, jumping with words and letters.

*

Later that evening, alone in her room, Akeelah slowly wrote "schottische" under "nociceptor" and "brunneous" in a thick notebook filled with handwritten words, a pink Post-it taped to the front cover. It said: *Property of Akeelah Anderson. Private and confidential. Do not open.* Everyone in the family had honored her request except Kiana, who took a peek one day while Akeelah was at school. One look was enough. She was greeted with a stream of words, none of which she understood. Terrence had never been inside her room and had no interest in anything his little sister did, said, or thought.

Akeelah grabbed the massive Webster's Unabridged Dictionary, which she had inherited from her father, its dog-eared pages filled with her notes and Post-its, and found the word that kept running through her mind.

"'Brunneous,'" she said out loud. "'Dark brown, used chiefly scientifically'...Well, why can't they just say 'brown'?"

She closed the dictionary and looked up at a framed photograph of her father, a gentle-looking man with a warm smile.

"You ever heard of these words, Daddy?"

She smiled at his image. "Yeah, you probably did." She stared into her father's eyes and then, against her will, remembered the scene from three years earlier that recurred again and again, both in her dreams and when awake. A game of Scrabble was in progress. Her father was hunched over the board, thinking. Akeelah was waiting for him to line up his word. Her father had taught her Scrabble the year before and she had immediately fallen in love with forming words and combinations of words. He smiled up at her before making his word. During the game he went out to the corner deli for a pack of cigarettes. Half an hour later, when he hadn't returned, Tanya began pacing the living room nervously. She knew the neighborhood and feared it.

Akeelah's smile faded as she remembered. It could have been yesterday, the scene was so vivid—the sound of gunshots from the street, the wail of police sirens growing louder. Those sounds haunted her mind now. And those memories triggered another: the sound of pounding on the front door, a somber-looking police officer on the front porch, her mother with a piercing cry knocking over a lamp that smashed to the floor.

Akeelah jerked suddenly in her seat. Returning to the present, her breathing ragged, she stared at her father's photograph. Her eyes filled with tears. "God, I miss you," she whispered. "You left us and we couldn't let you go. We still can't let you go. You're in every corner of the house. Your voice—your spirit—they're everywhere, Daddy. You understood…you understood everything."

She removed her glasses, damp from her tears, and wiped them absently on the sleeve of her blouse. Then she went to the window and slammed it shut, muffling the sounds of the neighborhood. She grabbed her word list and started methodically spelling words out loud. "'Anachronism.' A-n-a-c-h-r-o-n-i-s-m. 'Assiduous.' A-s-s-i-d-u-o-u-s…." The spelling, as it always did, had a calming effect on her. She was safely tucked in a world of her own, with her nonthreatening friends—letters and words that never bullied or belittled her. Bad images of the past evaporated. Her mind was at rest.

Three

The following morning when Akeelah arrived at Crenshaw Middle School, the exterior walkway was clogged with students. When the bell rang the students began slowly drifting to class, except for a few habitual truants, mostly male. Akeelah didn't hurry, either. She leisurely strolled up to a water fountain. Two of the toughest girls in her class, Myrna and Elaine, walked up behind her.

"Hey, freak," said Myrna, who was built like a football lineman. As Akeelah turned to find Myrna towering over her, the girl gave her a shove.

"How's the genius today?"

"I'm fine," Akeelah said. "And I ain't no genius."

"Oh yes, you are. Everybody know you are."

"No, I ain't."

"Me and Elaine, we want for you to take care of our English homework. Everybody call you a brainiac."

Akeelah shook her head emphatically. "Well, everybody is wrong. I ain't no brainiac."

"Like hell you ain't," Elaine said menacingly.

"Don't be tryin' to fool us," Myrna said. "You're always pullin' down A's."

Akeelah tried to twist away from the girls, but they grabbed her and started punching her face and shoulders.

Coming down the hall at that moment, as Akeelah fought the bigger girls with all the fury in her tiny body, was the school principal, Mr. Welch. Conservatively dressed in a dark suit and white shirt, grave and sanctimonious in manner, he was deep in conversation with a tall, somber African American in his mid-forties. With his tweed jacket and black turtleneck, he was the perfect model of a professor. All he lacked was a pipe.

"I can't tell you how much I appreciate your coming here today, Josh," Mr. Welch was saying. "The district's been breathing down my neck. Test scores dropped again last semester."

Dr. Joshua Larabee nodded, his lips pressed together. "Well, I appreciate your dilemma, but I don't think there's much I can offer."

"I just think if you see the kids in action you'll change your mind. I honestly think you will. Some of them are very special."

As they turned the corner, they came upon Akeelah fending off Myrna and trying to butt Elaine in the stomach with her head.

"Girls!" Mr. Welch shouted, "Why aren't you in class?" Dr. Larabee looked at the melee in dismay.

"She holdin' us up," Myrna said, nodding her head at Akeelah.

The two girls scampered off and when Akeelah started to follow them, the principal called out to her. "Akeelah—wait!"

She stopped and slowly turned around. Mr. Welch scrutinized her carefully. "What was that all about?"

She shrugged. "It wasn't nothin'. Just a little misunderstanding."

"I don't associate you with rowdy behavior," he said.

She shrugged again and stared at her shoes. She was very aware of the tall stranger but hadn't once glanced at him.

"Are you signed up for the school spelling bee today?" Mr. Welch went on.

"No."

"Why not?"

"I don't know."

"That's hardly an answer."

"Well, it's the only one I've got." She raised her eyes to his and managed not to flinch.

Mr. Welch said gravely, "Please come to my office. There are a few things we need to discuss."

The two men and Akeelah, who was fighting hard to maintain her composure, walked down the hall in silence. As Akeelah stood in front of the principal's desk, leaning first on one leg, then the other, Dr. Larabee studied some class pictures on the wall. Mr. Welch was poring over Akeelah's file.

"Well," he said, looking up finally, "Ms. Cross has an interesting record on you. According to her, you've never missed a word on your spelling tests."

Akeelah was aware that the tall man had turned to look at her. She could feel his gaze.

Mr. Welch cleared his throat and tried to catch her eye. "Your attendance record, however, leaves a little to be desired." He cleared his throat again. "More than a little, as a matter of fact." He studied her, waiting for a response, but she said nothing. "You're only eleven, according to your records. Did you skip a grade?"

Speaking to the edge of the desk, Akeelah said reluctantly, "The second."

"Why was that?"

"The work was too easy. That's what they told my mother." After a moment she added: "I wanted to stay with my class."

She glanced at Dr. Larabee for the first time as he took a seat beside the principal's desk. There was something in his eyes—an intensity, a depth, an intelligence—that reminded her of her father. He looked at her and then quickly away. He seemed bored with the whole affair, and jiggled his left leg, crossed over his right, impatiently.

"Akeelah," Mr. Welch said, "have you ever heard of the Scripps National Spelling Bee?"

Akeelah gave him a sudden intent look. "Uh...yeah....I saw some of it on TV last night."

"ESPN shows it every year," Mr. Welch said, leaning forward in his chair, a note of excitement in his voice. "Middle-schoolers from all over the country compete in school, district, and regional spelling bees, trying to make it to the National Bee. That's the goal, and the competition is keen." He paused until Akeelah felt compelled to look at him. He then continued, saying, "I have a dream for this school. That one of our students will be there. Whoever wins our school bee today will represent Crenshaw at the District Bee next month."

Akeelah stared at him but said nothing.

"Well? What do you have to say?" He smiled tentatively. "Have I made a convincing case?"

"Why would anyone wanna represent a school that can't even put doors on the toilet stalls?"

Dr. Larabee looked at her sharply, revealing the ghost of a grin for just an instant.

"You have to learn to take pride in what you have," Mr. Welch said, trying to cover his embarrassment. "Look, Akeelah…if we can't show that our students know how to perform and perform well, there might not be money for books, let alone bathroom doors. Do you understand me?"

Akeelah slowly nodded.

"Now I want you to do that spelling bee today. I can't order you to, but I really *want* you to. Will you do that for the school?"

Akeelah drew in a deep breath, sneaked a look at Dr. Larabee, and said, "Why should I? So everybody can call me 'freak' and 'brainiac' and attack me in the hall or on the way home?" She shook her head. "Naw, Mr. Welch. I ain't down for no spelling bee."

The principal glowered at her.

"Well, then, maybe you'd be 'down' for spending the rest of the semester in detention for all your absences." Akeelah and Mr. Welch locked stares. Dr. Larabee studied them both, his eyes suddenly alive with interest.

"Let me think about it," she said finally. "I'll come back here at lunchtime." She turned and marched stiffly out of the office.

The Crenshaw Middle School Spelling Bee took place that afternoon. The auditorium was sparsely filled, but nonetheless resounded with noisy, rowdy students. Akeelah, one of twenty contestants onstage, stared at the floor, her hand tapping nervously on her leg. Georgia waved to her from the first row and Akeelah grinned before looking away. Ms. Cross sat at a table on the side of the stage, and two other teachers served as assistant judges.

Ms. Cross approached the front of the stage as the audience began to settle down. She said, "Hello, and welcome to Crenshaw's first schoolwide spelling bee. We have some very special students competing today, so let's give them a big round of applause."

The clapping was scattered, and there were some sarcastic hoots and raspberries mixed in. Elaine and Myrna made faces at Akeelah, and Myrna shook her fist at her, mouthing some threatening words. A few rows back from the stage Mr. Welch sat with Dr. Larabee, talking earnestly into his ear. Dr. Larabee didn't look thrilled to be there.

"We drew numbers to see who'd go first," Ms. Cross went on, "and that would be Chuckie Johnson from the eighth grade. Chuckie—will you come up here to the mike?"

A plump boy strolled slowly up to the microphone. His buddies shouted out to him from the audience, and he waved to them and grinned. He then turned to Ms.

Cross and said, in a voice verging wildly between soprano and baritone, "Hey, what up?" His buddies broke into raucous laughter and Chuckie did a low comic bow.

"Now, Chuckie, you're going to start things off with 'grovel.' Okay? 'Grovel.'"

"'Grovel'?" Chuckie said. "Like, ya know—little rocks?"

"No," Ms. Cross said. "'*Grovel.*' Like get down on your knees and beg for mercy."

"Get down on my *knees?*" Chuckie said, completely confused. "Say what?"

"Just spell the word," the teacher said, trying to hide her growing impatience.

"*Okay,*" Chuckie said. "Uh…g-r-a-v-e-l?"

Akeelah rolled her eyes and then looked out at Dr. Larabee, whose gaze was fastened on her.

"Actually," Ms. Cross said, "it's g-r-*o*-v-e-l. Sorry, Chuckie. Better luck next time."

"Who cares? I didn't want to do this in the first place."

He rushed off the stage and joined his buddies.

"Okay, moving right along," Ms. Cross said, trying for a smooth and cheerful approach to a difficult job, "next up is Akeelah Anderson. Akeelah—would you step forward?"

She slinked up to the mike, her eyes fastened on the floor. She tried to ignore Georgia's whistles of encouragement and a few scattered catcalls.

Ms. Cross said, "Okay, Akeelah. Your word is 'doubt.' 'Doubt.'"

In a barely audible voice, Akeelah said, "'Doubt.' D-o-u-b-t."

"I'm sorry? You have to speak up. Talk directly into the mike."

Akeelah nodded, cleared her throat, and said, "D-o-u-b-t," her voice trembling but louder.

"Uh…very good."

Akeelah returned to her seat, her eyes cast down.

Mr. Welch nervously turned to glance at Dr. Larabee, who was watching the proceedings without expression.

"The words are pretty basic," the principal said.

Dr. Larabee nodded but said nothing.

"Next up, Regina Baker," Ms. Cross said.

Twenty minutes later, the competition had been reduced to two girls—Akeelah and Cheryl Banks, an eighth-grader. Cheryl was a rotund 200 pounds of intelligence and good cheer, picked on unmercifully by the girls in her class.

"Cheryl," Ms. Cross said, "your word is 'placid.'"

"'Placid.' That mean like remainin' calm? Take things as they come?"

"Exactly," she said. "An excellent definition."

"'Placid,'" she said. "Ah…p-l-a-s-i-d. 'Placid'?"

Akeelah shook her head as though to say, These words are just too easy.

"I'm sorry," Ms. Cross said. "It's p-l-a-c-i-d. Okay, Akeelah, if you get this next word you'll be the winner of the Crenshaw School Bee."

Moving to the microphone, she muttered under her breath, "Let's get this farce over with."

"The word is 'fanciful,'" she said. "'Fan—"

Akeelah interrupted her and said quickly, "F-a-n-c-i-f-u-l. 'Fanciful.'"

"Outstanding, Akeelah! You have won Crenshaw's inaugural spelling bee. Good job!"

Georgia cheered, as did Mr. Welch. Dr. Larabee, however, sat stony-faced, clearly not impressed.

Akeelah grabbed her blue ribbon and started to exit the stage when a high-pitched whistle suddenly cut through the room. All eyes in the auditorium swung toward Dr. Larabee, who stopped whistling and, to Mr. Welch's amazement, stood up.

"She's not done yet," Dr. Larabee said, staring at Akeelah intently. He leaned on the chair in front of him, took a deep breath, and speaking very slowly, said, "'Prestidigitation.'"

Laughter erupted at the size and complexity of the word. Akeelah stayed rooted in one spot, her hand beginning to beat against her thigh, her lips moving, as she stared suspiciously at the tall stranger.

"I'm sorry, sir…whoever you are," Ms. Cross said. "This girl is only eleven years old…and she's already won—"

"'Prestidigitation,'" Dr. Larabee repeated, cutting the teacher off. "Can you spell it?"

Akeelah's eyes stayed fixed on Dr. Larabee's; he looked steadily back at her. It was almost as though this middle-aged man and eleven-year-old girl were involved in a contest of wills.

Akeelah's hand continued to beat against her thigh. Sharply and suddenly she said, "P-r-e-s-t-i-d-i-g-i-t-a-t-i-o-n. 'Prestidigitation.'"

A stunned hush fell over the room. Even Chuckie Johnson and his rowdy friends were silent. Did she get it right? Even Ms. Cross, staring hard at Dr. Larabee, wasn't certain.

"That's correct," Dr. Larabee said, his voice neutral and quiet.

Georgia stood on her chair and let out a war whoop.

"'Ambidextrous,'" Dr. Larabee said, his eyes continuing to bore into Akeelah.

"Sir, these words are not appropriate for—" Ms. Cross began.

Akeelah cut in, saying, "A-m-b-i-d-e-x-t-r-o-u-s. 'Ambidextrous.'"

Her nervous hand tapped in rhythm as she spoke each letter. A hush had fallen over the room. The students had a hard time accepting that mousy little Akeelah Anderson could handle the words that Dr. Larabee machine-gunned at her. They were reduced nearly to silence, heads turning first to Dr. Larabee, then to Akeelah, as though they were watching a tennis match.

"'Pterodactyl,'" Dr. Larabee said next.

"P-t-e-r-o-d-a-c-t-y-l," Akeelah responded promptly.

Dr. Larabee nodded just perceptibly. "'Pulchritude,'" he said.

"P-u-l-c..."

Akeelah hesitated and looked down at her hand,

34

which had stopped tapping on her thigh and had begun to shake.

"Uh…r-i-t-u-d-e. 'Pulchritude'?"

A moment passed before Dr. Larabee said, "That's incorrect. It's from the latin root 'pulcher,' meaning beautiful. There's an 'h' after the 'c.'"

A painful pause filled the audience, followed by a faint collective sigh, as though the air had been sucked out of the room.

"See? She ain't so damn smart," Myrna said. That caused some of the students to laugh, partly as a relief from tension, partly to cover their embarrassment for Akeelah, who stood at the microphone looking mortified. She then bolted from the stage and out the side door of the auditorium, close to tears. Mr. Welch took the same exit and caught up with her halfway down the block.

"Akeelah," he shouted. "Wait! Where are you going? You did absolutely *great*. You were spelling words I can't even spell."

She pushed forward, half running. "Mr. Welch, I told you I didn't want to do this. They're all laughing at me now."

"They laugh because you intimidate them….They don't know what else to do."

"They laugh because they take me for a freak."

"I don't think so."

Mr. Welch and Akeelah turned to see Dr. Larabee taking long strides to catch up with them. He fell in step beside them. He stared hard at Akeelah, then turned to

Mr. Welch. "I'll give some consideration to what you've asked." With that, he spun on his heel and walked away.

Mr. Welch brought his hands together and grinned. "Akeelah, do you know who that was? Dr. Joshua Larabee. He used to chair the English Department at UCLA. He and I went to college together. And get this—when he was a kid he went all the way to the National Spelling Bee. And now he's considering personally training you for the District Bee."

Looking straight ahead, Akeelah said, "Well, he better find somebody else 'cause I ain't doin' no more spelling bees. I'm sick of people lookin' at me like I'm some kind of bug. I just wanna be left alone."

"Akeelah...," Mr. Welch protested, but she stormed off, running down the street and around the corner.

Georgia joined her on the stoop of her house a few minutes later, dropped her book bag at her feet, and sat down with a sigh.

"Girl, you kicked some major booty on that stage today. I knew you was good, but *that good?*" She shook her head and whistled.

"Are you kidding? I couldn't spell 'pulchritude.'"

"Who can? Nobody I know."

"The really good spellers can. Believe me."

"But you knocked the other words right back at that dude."

"They were just trick words, Georgia. Everybody knows 'pterodactyl' starts with a 'p.' Don't be givin' me too much credit."

"Girl, if I could spell like you, I *know* I could be a flight attendant."

Akeelah gave her friend an odd look. "You can be whatever you set your mind to."

Georgia punched Akeelah softly on the shoulder. "That's advice maybe you should take your own self," she said.

*

Akeelah was nearly asleep when she heard "Keelie?" whispered in her ear. Through her drowsiness she recognized Devon's voice. She opened her eyes and stared up at him, blinking the tiredness from her eyes. Devon had a knapsack slung over one shoulder and wore USAF regalia. He knelt down beside her. She rubbed her eyes.

"Devon…you leavin'? You just got here."

"Gotta get back to the base. I think we're bein' transferred, and all leaves got cut short." He ruffled her hair. "Hey, your principal called Mama. He said you did real good in a spelling bee. Knocked the ball out of the park."

"I messed a word up."

"Everybody messes up once in a while."

"You only got one chance in a spelling bee."

"He also said you got an opportunity to go to a bigger contest next week."

"I don't wanna do it."

"Why not?"

"I dunno. It's just dumb, you know? Everybody's gonna be lookin' at me, the weirdo who spells words.

This black girl from Crenshaw thinkin' she can spell with those rich white brainiacs. And the worst thing is, there's gonna be tons of words I don't know."

Devon squeezed her cheek and looked into her eyes. "So you're scared, huh, baby sister? Well, how do you think I felt the first time I jumped from an airplane? My whole body said, Don't do it—you *can't* do it, Devon. No way, man. But sometimes your brain's gotta be smarter than your body."

"But I don't like my school, Devon. The truth is, I *hate* it. I don't see why I gotta do anything for them. All they've given me is a crummy education."

"Then do it for Dad," Devon said. "You know how he was about words. He'd have loved to see you do something like this."

Akeelah looked over at the picture of her father, her expression thoughtful.

"What'd Mama say about it?"

"Ah, you know how Mama is. She's got a million things to worry about and she worries about every one of them." He reached for Akeelah's face with two hands and tilted it up so that she was looking directly into his eyes. "Tell you what. Just do this contest—and if you make it all the way to D.C., I'll parachute down to see you."

She smiled as Devon kissed her good night. When he softly closed the door, Akeelah crept out of bed and sat down at her computer. She turned it on and brought up the Web site for the Scripps National Spelling Bee, with a picture of the victorious red-haired girl. Akeelah looked up from the screen and studied the photograph of her father, whose warm, intelligent eyes seemed to be staring back at her, encouraging her.

"You want me to do this, Daddy? You think I can do it? Part of me wants to, another part of me is afraid to, and I just don't know what to do. I know you're in heaven, so pray for me. Pray that I make the right decision...."

Akeelah looked back at the red-haired girl, inhaled deeply, and slowly shook her head up and down, her lips pressed together in determination.

Four

Well before classes started the following morning, Akeelah was waiting outside the principal's office. When Mr. Welch arrived, he waved her into his office and asked her to sit down, which surprised her. Students usually stood through interviews with the principal.

"I've decided to keep on with the bee," she said before he'd had time to close the door.

Mr. Welch broke into a wide grin and vigorously pumped her hand.

"I think you've made an excellent decision," he said. "An excellent decision." He lowered his voice to a confidential whisper. "I don't think I have to tell you that you're Crenshaw's best hope to advance."

Akeelah nodded. "You think maybe the school could buy me a new outfit for the District Bee? I sure could use it." With a shy smile she added, "You don't want me to be a poster child for poverty, do you? We have to dress up Crenshaw a little."

"Uh, well, maybe if you make it to the State Regional Bee, something could be arranged. But you need to finish in the top ten at the district level first. And, Akeelah, you're going to be up against kids from Santa Monica, Woodland Hills, Beverly Hills. Some of them have been doing this for years and never even made it to D.C."

"You're not very encouraging, Mr. Welch." With an elaborate sigh, she added, "I've heard better motivational speeches."

"I'm just trying to stress the realities. I—we—we all have great belief in you."

"I don't know. Maybe I should just give up now."

"I'm not expressing myself very well, Akeelah. I'm just saying you're going to need to train hard—with Dr. Larabee."

Akeelah shook her head emphatically. "Uh-uh. I don't need no help from him. I can do this by myself."

"But, Akeelah, he knows all sorts of tricks and short-cuts. Besides, it would be good for both of you. He's been on a sort of…uh, sabbatical for a while. Anyway, he doesn't live too far from here. It could be convenient for you. Why don't you just go talk to him? You've got nothing to lose."

Mr. Welch handed her a sheet of notebook paper with Dr. Larabee's address. Akeelah studied it and then looked up. "He lives in this neighborhood? I thought you said he was important."

"And take this," Mr. Welch said, handing her a package. "It's a videotape of last year's National Bee."

Akeelah looked at the package and Dr. Larabee's address. Then up at the principal.

"Professor Larabee's kinda scary, Mr. Welch. I don't think he likes me."

"It's just his manner. He's really a very kind man. And an exceptionally intelligent one."

Akeelah struggled with the words for what she wanted to say next. She said finally, "The thing is, I'm just generally scared." Her voice was barely above a whisper. "The one thing I hate more than anything is standing out. Kids hate you for that. And—and the other thing is, am I good enough for this? Is this just a foolish, stupid pipe dream?"

"I don't think so."

"I wish I was as sure as you, Mr. Welch."

"It's normal to be scared, Akeelah. Just do your best. That's all anybody can ask of you—including you."

Akeelah nodded and looked up at him with a weak smile. "And don't forget about that new outfit if I get through the District Bee. I don't wanna be up onstage lookin' like the Patchwork Girl of Oz."

*

That night Akeelah sat in front of the living room TV watching last year's National Bee. A small, blond-haired boy wearing thick glasses was at the mike.

"'Solivagant,'" he said, repeating the word the Pronouncer had given him. "Can I have the language of origin, please?"

"The derivation is Latin," the Pronouncer said.

The blond boy nodded, his lips pressed together in thought.

"Is it derived from the Latin root 'vagus,' meaning to wander around?"

"Man," Akeelah said aloud, "these kids sure ask a lotta weird questions. Sound like a bunch of show-offs." Frustrated, she fast-forwarded through the tape, the words jumping out at her: "strophulus," "murenger," "xanthoma," "bhalu," "tichorrhine."

Her brother Terrence came up behind her and grabbed the back of her neck.

"Wass 'at?" he said, nodding his head at the TV.

She turned with a start. Her fourteen-year-old brother was dressed all in black and was wearing a thick gold chain around his neck—his adopted gang look.

"Where you been?" Akeelah said. "Mama's worried out of her mind."

"Mama always worried," Terrence said, clicking his tongue in annoyance. "She need to chill. Whatchu lookin' at?"

"Spellin' bee."

"I heard 'bout dat. You goin' up against a buncha rich white kids. You know what's gonna happen, don't ya? They gonna tear yo black butt up is what's gonna happen."

Akeelah shrugged and continued to stare at the screen.

"You hear me, girl?"

"I hear you, Terrence. You love to give advice. Now I'm gonna give you a little. Stay away from Derrick-T. He's bad news. You'll end up in real trouble if you stick with him."

"Derrick-T is the man," Terrence said. "Don't be rankin' on him."

"I'm just warning you."

"Okay, o*kay*, whatever. I've had enougha you for one night." Terrence turned away and head-bobbed and shoulder-swung his way to his bedroom.

"My brother don't believe in me," Akeelah whispered

under her breath. "Mama's too busy to care. And I'm all cramped up inside from big old doubts. But there's Devon—Devon and Daddy—they believe in me…." She snapped the video off, removed her glasses, and rubbed her eyes. "Now how 'bout tryin' to believe in yourself?"

*

The next afternoon, about thirty minutes after school let out, after frittering away fifteen minutes in the cafeteria drinking a soda with Georgia, Akeelah approached a large two-story house. It was unlike many of the grandiose houses in the neighborhood, which the owners had let slide into disrepair. In this place of declining hope and chronic despair, Dr. Larabee's house stood out. It symbolized pride. The lawn was immaculately cut, the garden blooming with flowers, the windows sparkling clean, and the wraparound porch freshly painted.

Akeelah checked the address, then slowly proceeded up the path to the porch, and after a moment's hesitation, rang the buzzer. She waited before ringing it again. There was still no answer. She then heard a clicking noise. Curious, she walked to the edge of the porch and peeked down the side of the house. She saw Dr. Larabee in the backyard on his knees, hammering something. She watched him for a moment and then climbed off the porch and walked down the path to the gate. She stood close by while Dr. Larabee, unaware of her presence, meticulously hammered a brick into the border of a well-maintained flowerbed.

He stopped, suddenly sensing that someone was

44

watching him. He looked up at Akeelah, his expression blank.

"You're late," he said.

"You didn't answer the door."

"That's because you're late."

"But I came right from school."

He checked his watch. "You must have dawdled."

"'Dawdled.' D-a-w-d-l-e-d."

"That's not funny," he said. "In fact, it's a little smart-alecky."

"Okay, I was talking to a friend and got held up a little."

Dr. Larabee nodded and then motioned for her to come into the garden area. She hesitated before opening the gate and stepping into the backyard. He returned to working on his garden.

"So you want to learn how to spell," he said, without looking up.

"I know how to spell."

That caused him to look up and study her closely. "No, you don't."

"Why do you say that?"

"You don't know how to spell with technique, language skills, memorization, and a mastery of strategies to correctly spell words you don't know how to spell."

She started to respond, but then simply nodded.

"Spell 'staphylococci.'"

Akeelah began tapping on her thigh until she seemed to lose the rhythm and paused. "Uh...s-t-a-f—"

"There's no 'f,'" he said. "S-t-a-*p*-*h*-y-l-o-c-o-c-c-i. It's derived from the Greek, so there can't be an 'f.' That was the winning word, National Spelling Bee, 1987. The first thing most serious spellers do is learn all the winning words. It's a crucial piece of strategy."

He walked over to a large plastic bag of soil.

"Well, maybe I ain't that serious," she said, her eyes burning into his back.

He paused, bent over the bag. "Then maybe I'm not serious, either."

He plunged a small spade into the bag and started sprinkling soil into the garden.

Akeelah watched him in silence for a moment. He was graceful and lithe for a large, muscular man, and she could sense his sensitivity underneath his grave exterior. Her father was the most sensitive man she'd ever known (he broke down crying when she swelled up from a bee sting when she was five years old and had to be rushed to the emergency room), but she felt that Dr. Larabee might run him a close second.

She continued to watch him until the silence grew uncomfortable. She said, "So why you home during the day? Ain't you got a job?"

He turned and looked at her sharply. "Do me a favor and leave the ghetto talk on the street. It bores me."

"Ghetto talk? What you mean by that? I don't talk *ghetto*."

"'Ain't'? I'm on to you, Akeelah. You use that word to fit in with your peers. As a matter of fact, you're way too concerned about fitting in and not nearly concerned enough about being who you are and taking pride in it.

You have to learn that settling for the lowest common denominator is a zero-sum game. Do you know the expression 'zero-sum game'?"

Akeelah shrugged. "There's no way to win."

"That's right. You win on one side but lose on the other, canceling out the win. When you're here with me, you speak correctly or don't speak at all. I insist on it." He regarded her closely. "That's the condition of working with me. Is that understood?"

"Yeah," she said after a pause. "Whatever."

"Whatever," he said, mimicking her, not looking pleased. He waved a hand toward the sidewalk. "You can leave now."

Akeelah stared at him and began tapping her foot nervously. "'Scuse me?"

"I said you can leave."

"How come? I just got here."

"I don't have the time or the patience for sullen, insolent children. Life is too short."

He turned away and resumed working on his garden.

"*Sullen?*" Akeelah said, her voice throbbing with indignation. "Insolent? I ain't—I mean, I'm *not*—sullen *or* insolent. It's just the first thing you do is start doggin' on my—criticizing the way I speak. I thought this was about spelling words. Sounds more like a personality makeover."

He kept working, not bothering to look up or acknowledge her.

"Hel*lo?* Dr. Larabee?" When he did not respond, she said, "Well, okay. That's fine. I'm outta here." She turned to leave but then stopped before going out the gate. "You know what? When I put my mind to it I can memorize anything. And you know something else? I don't need help from a dictatorial, truculent, supercilious...*gardener*. Sorry to be so insolent."

She marched down the path and out the gate, slamming it behind her.

Dr. Larabee looked up and slowly nodded his head. "Not bad, Akeelah," he muttered under his breath. "I'm impressed."

*

That night, bursting with a new determination fueled by Dr. Larabee's indifference, Akeelah pored over the Webster's Unabridged Dictionary. Tanya, wearing a nurse's uniform with white shoes and stockings, knocked lightly on her door.

"That you, Mama?"

"Yeah."

"Come on in."

Tanya stood framed in the door, concern etched on her face.

"Baby, why you still up?"

"Gotta learn more words," Akeelah said, her voice cracking with exhaustion. She let out a deep sigh. "You gonna come see me in the District Bee this Saturday?"

"It's at your school?"

Akeelah shook her head and grinned. "Nah. We're movin' up in the world. It's in Beverly Hills."

Tanya frowned and began tapping her foot, a habit Akeelah had unconsciously picked up from her.

"Beverly Hills?" Her daughter had vexed her, puzzled her, and occasionally delighted her and made her very proud from the time she was no more than a tot. Of her four children, Akeelah was the one she understood the least.

Tanya seemed to struggle with what to say next. "Look, you got other homework. You know you're way behind on things. I don't want you spendin' all your time on this game."

Akeelah reluctantly looked up from her computer. "It ain't a game," she said. "It's serious. So you gonna come see me in it?"

"Baby, you know I work at the hospital Saturdays. Maybe Kiana can go with you."

Akeelah let out an exasperated breath. "I guess that's okay if she don't bring that whiny baby with her."

"That baby happens to be your niece."

"I know what she is. I just know she'll start bawling when I'm in the middle of a word. That's the last thing I need. I'm already scared out of my mind."

Five

Early Saturday morning, Kiana brought her screaming baby out of the house and past Akeelah, who rolled
her eyes to the heavens. Mr. Welch's car, washed and
waxed for the occasion, was idling by the curb.

"Come on, girls," he called out. "We're going to be
late."

They piled in the car. As he roared away from the
curb, around the corner, tires squealing, Akeelah said quietly, "I don't think we're gonna be late, Mr. Welch. Either
on time or dead."

"I'm an excellent driver. Don't worry."

"Well, we're all prayin' you are."

When they arrived at Beverly Hills High (ten minutes
early, Mr. Welch announced proudly), more than a hundred middle school students and their parents were
crammed into the auditorium—a spacious and spotlessly
clean auditorium, Akeelah noted with envy. Many of the
parents were giving their children last-minute spelling
drills. Akeelah was dumbfounded, and more than a little
overwhelmed, at the number of kids entered in the competition.

"Dang," she said to Mr. Welch, "I didn't know there
would be *this* many."

"Don't worry about it," he said, squeezing her arm.

"Go get your number. We'll sit as close to the front as we can get." He smiled. "Break a leg, Akeelah."

She looked puzzled. "Break a leg?"

"That's an old saying in the theatrical world, wishing an actor good luck."

"Break a leg," she said, nodding. "That's funny." Akeelah eyed the baby apprehensively and said to her sister, "Maybe you shouldn't sit too close."

"Good luck, Keelie," Kiana said with a grin and a wink.

Looking numb and scared, Akeelah walked slowly up to a long table at the front of the auditorium, where volunteers handed out large-size numbers for the contestants to pin to their shirts.

"Name?" a volunteer said, smiling up at Akeelah.

"Akeelah Anderson."

The volunteer scanned the list and said, "Here you are, right here at the top. Hmm, I think you're the first speller we've ever had from Crenshaw Middle School."

Akeelah responded with a forced smile. "How many kids are entered in this thing?"

"One hundred thirty-nine."

"That many?" Akeelah shook her head, feeling way out of her league. One hundred thirty-eight against her. Well, no. She had a one in ten chance to make it to the next round, but still, the odds were overwhelming. She took her number, thanked the volunteer, and struggled to pin it to her shirt.

"Need some help?"

Akeelah turned to face a young Hispanic boy, about

her height, who had a cherubic face and a cheerful expression. He wore a hearing aid and his speech was slightly slurred.

"Javier Mendez," he said with a wide grin. "Twelve years old. Brilliant speller. Suave dancer. May I pin you?"

"Akeelah Anderson," she said with a giggle.

"Akeelah—that's a pretty name. Well, Akeelah, I'll try not to impale you. This your first time?"

"Yeah. Except for a bee at my school this week. You?"

"Second year. I made it to the Nationals last year. I finished thirteenth. *Lucky* thirteenth."

He struck a heroic pose and flexed his muscles. Akeelah began to realize that he was a bit of a clown. She also sensed that he was kind and she instantly warmed to him.

"You went all the way to D.C.?" she said.

"Yup. Three of us made it from my school, Woodland Hills. See that kid over there? His name is Dylan Watanabe." Javier pointed to a Japanese boy Akeelah recognized from the telecast of last year's National Spelling Bee. He was sitting next to his stern-faced father, listening attentively.

"Dylan's come in second place at the Nationals two years in a row. This is his last year of eligibility and everybody thinks he's gonna win. Frankly, I'd like to shove him off a steep precipice."

"That's good thinking," Akeelah said. "That way you get rid of the competition."

Javier gave a high-pitched giggle. "I like girls with a sense of humor. I hope you make the top ten."

"I hope I'm not the first one eliminated."

The Judge's voice boomed out over the PA system. "Will all the spellers take their assigned seats on the stage, please?"

"Ten-*hut*," Javier said, giving a mock salute. "Now remember"—he peered hard at her name pinned to her shirt—"Akeelah Anderson, if you don't know a word, spell it the way it sounds. Kids mess up all the time thinking they're being thrown a curveball when they're not. They outsmart themselves." He reached for her hand and they shook. "Good luck," he said.

"Good luck to you, too, Javier."

He started goose-stepping up to the stage and Akeelah could not help giggling. She nervously looked back at Kiana and Mr. Welch, who gave her the thumbs-up sign.

Moments later, all the contestants were seated except a twelve-year-old girl in pigtails at the microphone and the three spellers on deck standing behind her, including Javier and a very nervous Akeelah, who fiddled with her number.

"Your word is 'cacophony,'" the Pronouncer said.

The girl in pigtails smiled and said immediately, "C-a-c-a-p-h-o-n-y. 'Cacophony.'"

A bell dinged and the girl, dejected, dismounted the stage, her head bowed.

It was Javier's turn. He gave Akeelah a goofy grin before he did a half walk, half run up to the mike and faced the Judge, the Pronouncer, and several Assistant Judges. There was a faint tittering from the audience. Javier was clearly a crowd pleaser.

"Your word is 'rhesus,'" the Pronouncer said.

"'Rhesus'?"

Because of his speech impediment, Javier had to struggle to pronounce his words to the satisfaction of the judges. Javier simply accepted this as a challenge—life playing tricks on him—and he had learned at a very early age to compensate mightily. More often than not, he was the funniest boy in any group as well as the brightest.

"Try again," the Judge said. "Take your time."

"'Rhesus,'" Javier said with slightly more clarity. The Judge nodded. Javier rolled his eyes up, muttered something under his breath, and said, "Could I have a definition, please?"

The Pronouncer said, "A brownish-yellow monkey of India."

"Oh, *that* little fellow. 'Rhesus,' yes. R-h-e-s-u-s. 'Rhesus.'"

There was no bell. Javier started imitating a monkey as he returned to his seat, and drew a big laugh from the audience.

Now it was Akeelah's turn and she was petrified—too petrified to move, to think, even to breathe. She stared out at the sea of faces in the audience and they were a blur. Then an image of her father filled her mind. She could see his gentle eyes and feel his warm smile and hear his carefully chosen words as he told her that he was there for her, that he was watching. He spoke to her, saying, *You can do it, baby. I know you can do it. And I'm right here with you....*

"Number one-oh-eight," the Judge said.

Akeelah slowly rose to her feet, fought for a lungful of air, and stepped up to the mike.

"The word is 'eminent,'" said the Pronouncer. When she didn't respond immediately, the Judge said, "Did you hear the word?"

"Uh...I'm not sure if he's saying 'imminent' or 'eminent.'"

"Would you like a definition?" the Judge asked.

"That'd be cool," Akeelah said.

That brought a small ripple of laughter from the crowd, and Akeelah started tapping her foot nervously.

The Pronouncer said, "'Eminent.' Rising above other things or places; high; lofty....'Eminent.'"

"E-m-i-n-e-n-t," she said quickly. "'Eminent.'"

When there was no bell, she exhaled sharply and scampered back to her chair, relieved. Javier gave her an enthusiastic nod and a big grin.

Moments later, Dylan Watanabe sauntered up to the mike, all businesslike confidence, bordering on the arrogant. His word was "hypertrophic," which he spelled instantly, and then he returned to his seat without a smile or acknowledgment of the audience applause. Akeelah noticed that Dylan's father—arms crossed over his chest, expression grim—did not applaud.

Akeelah stepped up to the microphone for the next round.

"The word is 'concierge,'" the Pronouncer said.

She started tapping lightly on her thigh. "Uh...is that,

like, a guy who stands around in a hotel? Wears a uniform?"

"Speak into the mike, please," the Judge said.

"A concierge," said the Pronouncer, "is a head porter or doorkeeper. The origin is French."

Akeelah nodded as she continued to tap her leg. "C-o-n-c-i-e-r-g-e. 'Concierge.'"

As she returned to her seat. Javier leaned toward her and whispered, "You're doing great." He raised both of his thumbs.

"I'm gettin' mad lucky. I could be gettin' words like 'vinculum.' Really tricky words."

The speller at the mike put one too many "n's" in "vinculum," the bell went *ding!* and the speller left the stage, fighting back tears. Akeelah and Javier exchanged knowing glances.

Half an hour later, only a handful of spellers remained onstage. Many of the disappointed parents in the audience had left. For those remaining in the auditorium, the tension had grown more palpable.

The Judge approached the podium and spoke loudly into the mike. "As you can see, we're down to eleven spellers. The top ten qualify for the Southern California Regional Finals. So in the next round if you miss a word, please do *not* leave the stage...."

Suddenly the loud crying of a baby erupted from the sparse audience. Akeelah felt her stomach tighten. She shot a look at Kiana that could kill (she and Mr. Welch had moved closer to the stage) as Kiana tried to calm her child. But the crying soon turned to wailing.

Akeelah half rose from her chair and said in a kind of strangled shout, "Kiana, get that baby outta here."

Kiana huffed with indignation and threw up her free hand in protest before marching out of the auditorium with her screaming baby. Akeelah smiled sheepishly at the Judge, who looked unmoved.

"So let's begin," he said.

Fifteen minutes later, the eleven remaining spellers were still in contention. Javier was up and his word was "syllogize." He cocked his head to one side and stared at the ceiling, peered out at the audience, and milked the moment for all it was worth.

"Mr. Mendez," the Pronouncer said, with a hint of impatience.

Javier nodded and gave the Pronouncer a brilliant smile. "'Syllogize.' S-y-l-l-o-g-i-z-e."

His parents cheered as he gave a high sign and moonwalked over to the right side of the stage where the other finalists were congregated.

It was Akeelah's turn to step up to the mike. Kiana peeked through the small window in a door near the stage, watching her sister intently.

"'Synecdoche,'" said the Pronouncer.

Akeelah's hand froze on her thigh. "'Si-neck-do-key?' You wanna tell me what that means?"

"It is a figure of speech in which a part is used for a whole, an individual for a class, a material for a thing, or the reverse of any of these."

Akeelah stared at the Pronouncer for a moment, then let out a breath and leaned her head against the microphone, which made a popping sound. Her hand nervously tapped away, she blinked her eyes rapidly and cleared her throat. She saw Mr. Welch leaning forward in his chair, hopeful, seemingly willing her on. Then she caught sight of Dr. Larabee standing in the back, completely immobile, watching her intensely. She was surprised to see him and had to force herself to breathe. *Dissect it, girl,* she said to herself. *The problem is in the ending.*

"We need you to spell the word," the Judge said.

Akeelah nodded. She made a fist with her nervous hand, took a deep breath, and said, "S-y-n-e-c-d-o-k-e-y. 'Synecdoche.'"

The bell dinged, which to Akeelah's ears was the sound of doom. She glanced at Dr. Larabee, who was looking down, closed her eyes, and rocked back and forth as though she might fall to the floor. Utterly dejected, she walked with her head down to the left side of the stage and sat in one of the chairs, conspicuously alone—a loser on this side of the stage, with all the winners on the other side. When she dared look in Mr. Welch's direction, his expression was grim. *I screwed up, Daddy. I ruined everything. Why couldn't I spell that stupid word?* She fought back tears. The last thing she would allow herself was to reveal her wretchedness to the audience and the other contestants.

The final speller, a girl with spiky hair, nervously approached the mike.

"Your word is 'carmagnole,'" the Pronouncer said.

"If you spell this correctly," said the Judge, "you'll be our tenth and last finalist."

The girl nodded, looking frightened. Akeelah had shrunk into her seat as though she wanted to curl up and disappear—leave the earth and reappear as someone else. Kiana, with her face still pressed to the window of the door, concentrated on the spiky-haired kid, wanting to edge into her mind and will her to misspell the word.

"Could I get a definition?" she said.

"A lively song and street dance," said the Pronouncer.

The spiky-haired girl nodded but looked confused. She coughed and cleared her throat. "Uh…c-a-r…"

Kiana noticed that in the audience, the spiky-haired girl's mother was nodding to her in an encouraging manner. Kiana drilled her with her eyes.

"…m-a…," the spiky-haired girl continued.

She stopped and stared hard at her mother. She watched her mother nodding. But the girl was stuck, with no idea how to proceed. Then Kiana saw the woman mouth the letter "g."

The girl quickly spelled the rest of the word: "g-n-o-l-e."

"Congratulations!" said the Judge, joining the girl at the mike. "You are the tenth finalist in the LAUSD Spelling Bee."

Kiana shook her head and cursed under her breath. "No way. No *way*." She barreled through the door, holding the baby, and rushed onstage.

"*They cheated,*" Kiana yelled, scaring the baby into a fresh bout of crying. "I saw them! Her mama gave her the letter 'g.' She was sayin' 'Geeee'!"

All eyes in the audience were now turned to the mother.

"I didn't help her," the woman said, glaring at Kiana. "That girl is making it up."

"She's lying!" Kiana shouted. "I'm telling you she gave her daughter that letter. I saw her with my own two eyes."

"But she knew the word," the woman said, gesticulating wildly. "I mean—it's one we studied. She *knew* it!"

"Ma'am," the Judge said, his tone severe, "did you help your child spell the word? You have to understand this is a serious business."

The mother was now flustered, her voice shaking. "You're darn right this is serious. You're giving these kids ulcers with the tension, the stress—all the hours they spend learning to spell words. And they have all their other work to do—and—and they're driven crazy. You know how long she's been studying for this? I'm telling you, she would've gotten the word by herself. I was just trying to help. There was no actual cheating here."

Her daughter shook her head. "No, I wouldn't have gotten the word without your help. I didn't have a clue about the extra letter."

There was dead silence in the auditorium. The girl wiped her eyes and bowed her head. Then the Judge said, "I'm sorry, Number thirty-four. According to the rules, you're disqualified from the competition. Which means Number one-oh-eight"—he pointed to Akeelah—"you're the tenth finalist, and you're going to the State Regionals."

Akeelah stood there looking stunned and then slowly

rose to her feet. Soon she was surrounded by a proud Mr. Welch and a whooping Kiana.

"Way to go, girl," Mr. Welch exclaimed. "I knew you could do it."

"But I missed a word."

"It doesn't matter—we're in! Thank God for eagle-eye Kiana." He gave her a hug. The baby was finally sleeping peacefully—now that the contest is over, Akeelah thought to herself. Wouldn't you just know.

*

Moments later, as Akeelah and Javier moved toward the exit, he handed her a piece of paper.

"Here's my number," he said. "We've got a spelling club at my school. You should come and practice with us sometime."

"That sounds like fun."

"You're good, Akeelah. You really are. I think you've got a great chance to get to D.C."

"I sure hope you're right. I've got a lot to learn."

"We all do," Javier said, showing a new seriousness. "The thing about spelling is, there's no end to the learning. Sometimes I feel like I'm one yawning pit of ignorance."

"Me, too. I feel exactly that way."

"Hey, there's my folks," he said. "I'll catch you later."

Javier scurried off with his parents, leaving Akeelah waiting for Mr. Welch to finish chatting with the Judge. Suddenly Dr. Larabee was looming over her. It was impossible to read his expression.

"Why didn't you ask if 'syn' was the Greek root meaning 'with or together'?"

"Excuse me?"

"Or 'ekdoche,'" he continued, "meaning 'interpretation.' Syn-ecdoche. The only difficult word you were given all day and you missed it."

"Well, maybe if I had a coach I woulda done better. I'm really surprised you're here. I thought you didn't have time to waste on this kinda thing."

"You're wrong. I have all the time in the world for someone with talent who wants to learn. What I don't have time for are rude little girls." He paused and then said, "Spelling bees are terrific entertainment, don't you think?"

"Yes. But more for the audience than the speller."

He nodded. "Anyway, good luck to you. You'll need it."

He put on his hat and walked out of the auditorium. Akeelah stood there, tapping her foot and looking perturbed.

Six

Mr. Welch drove back to South Los Angeles, much more slowly than earlier, in an ebullient mood. He had bought double-dip ice cream cones for Kiana and Akeelah (chocolate for Kiana, vanilla for Akeelah), and they were busy licking them in the backseat and replaying the bee.

"That little Hispanic kid," Kiana said. "You like him?"

"Javier Mendez," Akeelah said. "He's nice. Really a cool kid."

"Seems like a funny little dude. He kind of makes you smile."

"He invited me to join his spelling group in Woodland Hills."

"Whoa. Look at li'l sister, movin' up in the world."

"I need to do anything I can to improve my spelling skills."

"You're right," said Mr. Welch enthusiastically. "You've got the right attitude, Akeelah."

She sighed. "What bothers me is, I'm only movin' on because that woman cheated." She reached for Kiana's hand and squeezed it. "You made it happen."

"A little luck never hurt nobody."

"I second that," Mr. Welch said. He drove in silence

63

as they entered their neighborhood—back to a big dose of reality, Akeelah said to herself—then he said, "Just think, Akeelah, if you can place in the top three at the State Regionals, you'll go all the way to D.C. How great would that be!"

"It won't happen if I can't spell 'synecdoche.'"

"Uh-oh, look," Kiana said, pointing out the window.

A police car was parked in front of their house, its lights flashing. Two police officers were taking handcuffs off Terrence. He looked mildly bored. They walked him up to the porch where Tanya was waiting for him, hands on hips.

The police drove away, after a quick conversation with a very annoyed Tanya. The two sisters thanked Mr. Welch for the ride and cautiously approached the porch, where Tanya had Terrence by the arm and was shouting at him. He hung his head but his face was a blank, as though he were somewhere far away.

"As long as you're living in *my* house you're gonna do as I say. That means *no* drugs, *no* gangbangers—and *no* *three-hundred-dollar watches*. It's my way or the highway, Terrence, and you better believe I'm dead serious." She punctuated her angry outburst by ripping the watch off Terrence's wrist.

"Hey," he said. "Chill out, will ya? Derrick-T gave that to me. What are you doin'?"

"I'm giving it back." Aware of the girls, she waved a hand toward the front door. "You two go inside."

"Mama, I made it," Akeelah said.

Tanya looked at her blankly. "Made what?"

"The cut," Akeelah said. "At the District Bee? I'm goin' to the State Regionals."

"You're what?" Tanya was torn between disciplining Terrence and listening to Akeelah. "Well, fine," she said, without enthusiasm. "But while you're off doing these spelling bees, we might be visiting your brother in the morgue." Suddenly she turned on Terrence and slapped him across the face.

He backed up a step and held a hand to his cheek. "Why'd you do that? You're one crazy lady, you know that?"

She grabbed Terrence by the arm and dragged him into the house, followed closely by Kiana, leaving Akeelah standing out on the porch alone. She shook her head sadly, then slowly entered the house and locked the door. Akeelah could hear Tanya and Terrence continuing to argue in the living room. She went into her room and plopped down at her desk, trying to block out the shouting. She looked at the picture of her father.

"Guess what, Daddy? I'm going to the State Bee. I might not get no further, but at least that's something, isn't it? I think it is." She smiled, then looked up as a police siren passed by the house, followed by the piercing wail of an ambulance rushing to the usual South Los Angeles disaster, mixed in with the sounds of Tanya and Terrence shouting at each other in the next room.

Akeelah's eyes returned to the photograph of her father. His eyes seemed to stare back into hers. She nodded, as though something of importance had passed between them. She lay on her bed fully clothed and closed her eyes.

"'Synecdoche,'" she said in a whisper. "S-y-n-e-c-d-o-c-h-e...."

*

The next day, Akeelah sat in a window seat on a bus, looking out at the streets passing by. In her lap was a city map on which she had marked out the bus routes leading to Woodland Hills. She had Googled Woodland Hills the night before and the information she downloaded confirmed what she already knew: the community where Javier lived was a world removed from South Los Angeles. It was a community of well-maintained houses and well-run schools. It was a rich community, full of professional people—doctors, lawyers, and entertainers.

It was a place that, most of all, existed only in Akeelah's dreams and fantasies.

She had skipped her afternoon classes to take Javier up on his invitation. She had brought along a copy of *The Catcher in the Rye* but was too excited to open it. Through the window she watched South Los Angeles become Mid-Wilshire become Koreatown become Hollywood. When the bus entered the Valley, Akeelah's nose was to the window as she tried to take in the changing scene as it went by in a blur. She watched Studio City become Sherman Oaks become Encino. She was bemused by a group of rich white teenage girls who passed the bus in a convertible BMW, bouncing their heads to a rap song.

The bus deposited Akeelah directly in front of the Woodland Hills Middle School. It was clean, well maintained, and affluent—a dream school, Akeelah thought. The kind of place you would be eager to go to each morning. The kind of place where you would love to learn.

She slowly entered the school grounds, went in the main door, along with some stragglers rushing back from lunch (the bell for class had already rung), and walked down the school's center hall. She noticed that most of the kids were white, but there were some minority students— black, Hispanic, and Asian. She examined the students, looking for a familiar face. She spotted Dylan Watanabe through the open door of a classroom, seated behind a chemistry lab station. He was writing down numbers from a series of thermometers in four containers of liquids. Akeelah watched him for a moment before quietly approaching him.

"Dylan?"

He looked up to see her standing in front of him.

"Hi," she said. "My name's Akeelah Anderson. I was in the District Bee with you last week."

Dylan hesitated and then said, "I remember." His tone was cool and distant. He quickly looked away from her and returned to his work.

"Uh…Javier said I could come and join your study group today. I hope that's okay."

He waved a hand dismissively. "All the rejects do that. My father coaches me privately. Who's your coach?"

"I don't got one."

"You don't *have* one?" he said, deliberately correcting

her grammar. He sized her up, from head to toe. "How many spelling bees have you won?"

"Just the one at my school. I've only been in two bees."

He continued to stare at her and then said suddenly, "Spell 'xanthosis.'"

"Ah...z-a-n—"

"It starts with an 'x,'" Dylan said. "If that idiot girl hadn't been caught cheating, you wouldn't have made the cut. Give it up. I hate to break it to you, but you don't have what it takes."

Dylan disregarded her and started to pack up his stuff. Stricken, feeling sick to her stomach, Akeelah ran out of the classroom. She rushed through the crowds of students, making a beeline for the front gate. She had made a mistake, a stupid, awful mistake. She didn't have what it takes—that's what Dylan had told her and she knew he was right. She would wait for the next bus and go back to her own neighborhood, where she belonged.

"Akeelah!"

She stopped and turned to see a smiling Javier approaching.

"Hey, my mom told me you called. I'm glad you could make it."

Dylan came out of the chemistry lab at that moment, saw Akeelah and Javier together, chuckled, and walked on.

"He said I don't have what it takes," Akeelah said, on the verge of tears.

"Don't listen to Dylan Watanabe. He's a jerk. Come on...."

He took Akeelah by the hand and led her down the walkway. "We have this game we do while we spell. You'll love it."

A bunch of students, all spellers, were congregated at the basketball court.

"'Euphoric,'" Javier said and passed the basketball to a frizzy-haired twelve-year-old girl named Polly.

"It's an adjective," Polly said. "The origin is Greek."

She passed the ball to Roman, a short, chubby thirteen-year-old.

"It means, like, feeling great and everything."

The ball then went to Akeelah, who stood under the basket, not sure what to do.

"You either spell the word," Javier said, "or take a shot. If you miss either one, you get a strike. Three strikes you're out."

She looked up at the basket, feeling doubtful, and said, "'Euphoric.' E-u-p-h-o-r-i-c."

She sensed that the others seemed impressed and she began to feel a little better. She passed the ball to Javier and said, "'Psoriasis.'"

"It's a noun, origin Greek. Are you taking Latin at your school?" He passed the ball to Polly.

"Are you kidding? My school's barely got enough money for kickballs. There's no Latin class. You wanna know how bad it is? Half the bathrooms don't work."

"That really sucks," Polly said. "Latin really helps you understand words. Uh…'psoriasis' is, like, itchy skin." She passed the ball to Roman.

Javier looked at Akeelah, no longer smiling. "Maybe

69

your mom could drive you up here so you can take some classes with us."

"I don't know," Akeelah said. "To be honest, this is all startin' to sound real heavy."

"It *is* heavy," Roman said. "Spelling bees are serious. I think I'll take a shot."

He tried a two-handed shot, the old-fashioned way, and it fell woefully short of the basket.

"On second thought," he continued, "could I spell the word?"

*

When they completed the workout, Akeelah walked with Javier to the main parking lot, where parents were picking up their kids. The cars ranged from a Mercedes to a Subaru—nothing further down the car chain than a Subaru. The mothers, for the most part, were slender and well groomed. And white. Akeelah tried not to feel intimidated by the kind of suburban glamour she had seen only in movies.

"This is so different from my school," she said. "At Crenshaw they think I'm a *freak*."

"Don't kid yourself. They think we're freaks here, too. Maybe they're just a little more polite about it."

"Really?"

"Big time. Hey, there's my mom. You need a ride?"

She saw Javier's mother waiting for him in a silver Mercedes.

"Nah," Akeelah said. "My mom's gonna pick me up. She should be here soon."

"Okay. Hey, I almost forgot. I'm havin' a birthday party in a few weeks. You wanna come?"

"I don't know if I can. I'll let you know."

Javier's mother beeped her horn and gave Akeelah a smile and a wave.

"Ask your mom. I really hope you can come to my party."

"It would be nice."

"It was cool seein' you again, Akeelah. Bye."

"Bye."

Javier smiled and rushed to his mother's car and climbed inside. Akeelah waited for the car to disappear around a corner and then crossed the street to the bus stop. The sun was sinking low in the sky as she boarded the bus back to reality. She replayed her confrontation with Dylan, deciding that even though he might be a talented speller, he was also a conceited jerk and not worthy of all the thought she was giving him. She smiled when she thought of Javier. He was one of the main reasons she felt that she could continue. She fell asleep on the last stretch of the journey. When the bus pulled up to a corner in her neighborhood, the driver woke her up and she practically sleepwalked to her house, unlocked the front door, and came face to face with a furious Tanya.

"Where on earth have you been, young lady? You better have a good explanation."

"I've been studyin'."

"Studying? Where have you been studying?"

"Woodland Hills," Akeelah said, stifling a yawn.

She tried to sidestep her mother, who grabbed her by the shoulder.

"*Woodland Hills?* What were you doin' there?"

"They got a spelling club and this kid invited me to join it. It's really good practice, Ma. I learned a lot today."

"Did Mr. Welch take you? Nobody called *me.*"

Akeelah hesitated, knowing that what she said next would not go down easily with her mother, but she was too tired to think up a creative lie. "I went by myself," she said. "I didn't think the bus would take so long. I'm sorry."

Tanya stared at her daughter, shaking her head.

"Akeelah Anderson, have you lost your mind? You're *eleven years old.* You don't take a bus to the Valley by yourself. For a bright girl, you certainly can be stupid sometimes."

"But there was nobody around to take me. You're never home during the day."

"That's because I'm at work tryin' to earn enough money to keep food on the table. I can't be traipsing off to no Valley on a whim."

"It ain't no whim."

"It is to me."

"It was the same thing on the weekend. You couldn't come. All the other kids had their parents at the District Bee."

"Well, maybe the 'other kids' got parents with time on their hands. Time and money. Now I will *not* have another child disappearing at all hours. One Terrence is enough. So if this spelling thing means sneakin' off to the suburbs by yourself, then you can just forget about it. We're calling it off."

"We can't call it off! I'm going to the Regional Bee."

"You think so?"

"I know so."

"Don't get smart with me, Akeelah. You're eleven and I'm still your mother."

"I'm going, Ma. I have to."

"Not if you flunk out of school you're not. I just got a letter that says you gotta take summer school to make up for all the classes you skipped."

"Summer school? But, Ma, I hate Crenshaw. It's boring, it's full of idiots, and nobody cares. I mean the students *and* the teachers."

"You think they care about you at Woodland Hills? You think all those rich white folks are gonna welcome you with open arms?"

"Well, at least they got Latin classes and the kids don't have to study in the stairwells. They're doin' things right at their school, and we ain't doin' *nothin'* right."

"Good for them," Tanya said. "Hur*ray* for them. But until you finish summer school at Crenshaw, where last I knew you're still a student, there's gonna be no more talk of spelling bees."

"But, Ma, the State Regionals happen *during* the summer."

"Then you're just gonna have to wait to do it next year. Getting a passing grade is more important than a buncha words."

"But that's not fair!"

"Not only is it fair," Tanya said, "it's final."

Beside herself with frustration and anger, Akeelah turned and stomped off to her room and flung herself down at her desk. She was seething now, all sleepiness gone. She looked at her father's picture, studied his face closely as she had done so many times before.

"You'd let me do it," she said out loud. "I know you would. You always encouraged me to do everything. 'Sky's the limit,' you used to tell me."

She sat there fuming for a long moment, looking at her father expectantly, as though she was waiting for him to talk, to ease her pain. Then it occurred to her what she needed to do. From her notebook she pulled out the parental consent form for the Southern California Regional Spelling Bee. She studied it and then looked up at her father's picture.

"You know I have to do this, Daddy. I don't have a choice."

She took a deep breath and slowly signed the bottom of the form, forging her father's careful handwriting.

Samuel Anderson....

Seven

Akeelah stood in front of Dr. Larabee's house the following Monday, the first day of summer vacation. She took a deep breath, muttered "Good luck, girl," then rang the buzzer. After a few moments, Dr. Larabee answered the door. They stared at each other for a moment, neither willing to start the conversation.

Akeelah said finally, "1979. 'Maculature.' M-a-c-u-l-a-t-u-r-e. 1990. 'Fibranne.' F-i-b-r-a-n-n-e. 1996. 'Vivisepulture.' V-i-v-i-s-e-p-u-l-t-u-r-e."

She took a breath. He looked at her, his head cocked to one side, the trace of a smile turning up the corner of his mouth.

"I learned all the winning words since 1924. Just like you said I should." She waited for him to respond, but when he didn't she rushed on, saying, "I'm sorry for being so insolent last time. That's not gonna happen no more—anymore. I promise." Again she waited for him to say something, but he didn't. "So I was wondering…I was wondering if you might reconsider coaching me for the State Bee. 'Cause I need a coach. Bad."

There was a long pause as he seemed to consider what she was proposing. Then he let out a long, deep breath.

"Badly," he corrected her. "You need a coach badly." He opened the door wider. "Come in."

He stepped back into the house, leaving the door half open behind him. Akeelah hesitantly ventured into the foyer and was immediately impressed by the antique wooden moldings and by how immaculate and well kept the house was. He might live in a bad neighborhood— her neighborhood—but his house was really cool.

"Wipe your feet," he said.

She turned back to the doormat and did as she was told. Dr. Larabee disappeared through an office door at the end of a long hall. Akeelah hesitated and then followed him. Swallowing back nervousness, she entered the impressive room flanked by two towering bookcases made of polished walnut. On the wall were framed university degrees from Yale and UCLA, as well as photographs of Dr. Larabee as a younger man on the Yale football team and with a pretty black woman with a dazzling smile.

Dr. Larabee moved behind his desk, every inch the professor. Standing hunched over his computer, he finished typing something and then, without looking up, said, "So tell me, Akeelah. What guarantee do I have that I can trust you?"

"'Scuse me?"

"I don't want to squander my time on someone who's not committed. Commitment is crucial for success. Work, hard work, work all the time, practically in your sleep. That's what it's going to take."

"Well, I'm committed."

He finally looked up at her, but she couldn't read the expression in his eyes. She thought she detected a hint of warmth.

"How do I know that? You're a very unpredictable little girl. Blowing warm, then blowing cold."

"All I can do is make you a promise," Akeelah responded calmly. "And if that's insufficient, well, I'm sorry, sir. All I have is my word."

She held Dr. Larabee's gaze as he slowly nodded. After a pause, he sat down behind his desk and gestured for her to take a seat. Akeelah saw a more recent photo of Dr. Larabee and the pretty woman with the dazzling smile.

"She's beautiful," Akeelah said, nodding at the wall. "She your wife?"

Ignoring her question, Dr. Larabee said, "Listen—you got lucky at the District Bee. You're aware of that, aren't you?"

She nodded. "I'm aware of it."

"The competition's much stronger at the state level. You're up against kids who have practiced for years, kids who can afford private tutors. So if we were to prepare for that, we'd do it on *my* schedule. I administer online classes in the afternoon"—he glanced at his computer— "so that means we'd work in the mornings. Can you handle that? You must know by now that I won't tolerate tardiness."

"Well, I'm supposed to have summer school, but Mr. Welch said workin' with you could take the place of it."

"Summer school? Isn't that for students who fail to perform satisfactorily during the year?"

"Yes," Akeelah said evasively. "But sometimes it's for kids who wanna get *ahead* for next year."

She smiled, but could tell he wasn't buying it. His eyes had that steely look that was a little scary.

"Do you have any goals in life?" he said. "Something you feel passionate about?"

"Huh?"

"*Goals.* What do you want to be when you grow up? A doctor? Lawyer? Stand-up comic? You're only eleven, but you must have given this some thought."

"I dunno. The only thing I'm good at is spelling."

Dr. Larabee studied her again at length.

"Go over there," he said. "To that plaque on the wall. Read what it says."

Akeelah hesitated and then walked across the room to a small brown plaque with an engraving on it. She started to read it to herself.

"Aloud," Dr. Larabee said. "Read it aloud."

"Uh…'Our deepest fear is not that we are inadequate. Our deepest fear is that we are powerful beyond measure.'" She frowned before going on, wondering if those words could be true. She had never seen fear that way. Fear diminished you, and it diminished you because it made you face your shortcomings. She was sure of it, and yet…. She continued to read: "'We ask ourselves, Who am I to be brilliant, gorgeous, talented, and fabulous? Actually, who are you *not* to be those things? Your playing small doesn't serve the world. We were born to make manifest the glory of God that is within us. And as we let our own light shine, we unconsciously give others permission to do the same.'"

She looked at Dr. Larabee, wondering what he would say, what he would ask her, how she would respond.

"It's a quote from Marianne Williamson's book *A Return to Love*. Does it mean anything to you?" he said.

"I don't know."

"Come on, Akeelah. It's written in plain English. What does it mean? You're an intelligent girl. Use your intelligence."

"That I'm not supposed to be afraid, I guess," she said.

"Afraid of what?"

"Afraid of…me?"

"You're close."

He waved. "Come here."

She approached his desk, tapping lightly on her thigh.

"This bee, this National Spelling Bee, it's a tough nut. You don't have any idea how tough it is. I've seen it chew kids up and spit them out. And if you want to get there, you can't be a shrinking violet. You have to stand up and show people what you can do. All right?"

Akeelah nodded.

"And I'll brook no nonsense," he continued. "You show up every day, on time. With no attitude. Otherwise it's over. Agreed?"

"Agreed."

"The quote was telling you that you're afraid of your potential. You have no need to be. If you work hard your potential will manifest itself, and my guess is, slowly you'll lose your fear. Think about it."

Dr. Larabee rose from his desk and said, "We start tomorrow. Nine a.m. sharp. You're going to learn to visualize words, because words are not ethereal. They're pictures. Pictures of ideas. And if you can see the picture, you can see the word."

*

On the day of Javier's birthday party, Kiana drove a nicely dressed Akeelah through Woodland Hills. Kiana had borrowed the car, an old red Mustang, from her current boyfriend. Georgia sat in the backseat, and they were listening to rap on the radio while Akeelah monitored the passing house numbers.

"Mama'd trip if she knew I borrowed the car from Maurice. She hates Maurice."

"Well, you got to admit, Kiana, he's a little slow on the uptake."

"I don't care about that. I don't need no rocket scientist. He's a good guy. That means a lot to me after the experiences I've had. Anyway, what Mama ain't gonna know ain't gonna hurt her."

"Stop!" Akeelah said suddenly. "Here it is."

Kiana pulled up to the curb in front of Javier's house, festooned with balloons. The house was a large white Colonial with four columns, and Georgia whistled. "That's some crib, girl," she said, nudging Akeelah. "These folks must be filthy rich."

Akeelah got out of the car, but Georgia was not budging. She looked warily at Javier's house—and the backyard party in full swing, mostly full of white kids.

"You coming, Georgia?"

"I guess I'll go to the mall with Kiana instead."

"I thought you were excited about this party."

Javier had spotted them and came running out from the backyard, waving his hand and grinning.

"Hey, Akeelah!"

"Okay, whatever," she said to Georgia. "I'll see you later."

Georgia looked uneasy as she watched Akeelah scamper off with Javier. She couldn't understand Akeelah's attraction to Woodland Hills and all these white kids. Their neighborhood wasn't much, but at least it was their neighborhood. It was where they belonged, where they felt comfortable and they were with their own kind.

In the backyard Javier introduced Akeelah around. A blindfolded young girl took a whack at a piñata with a baseball bat. A group of kids threw beanbags into a cardboard clown's mouth. Others played soccer, doing more screaming than kicking and ball-butting, and Dylan Watanabe deftly maneuvered the ball through his opponents.

Akeelah turned to Javier with a frown. "Why'd you invite *him?* You don't even like him."

They each had grabbed a slice of birthday cake and were eating at a table under a ginkgo tree.

"My dad's friends with his dad. I'm surprised he showed up. I know he's not exactly crazy about me."

"Hey, Javier," Roman shouted, "we need another player!"

"No, that's okay. Count me out. Old war injury." He tapped his hearing aid and grinned.

"You can't play 'cause of your hearing aid?" Akeelah asked.

"That's just an excuse. I suck at soccer. But the hearing aid gets me off the hook. Come on—I'll show you my house."

He took Akeelah by the hand and led her up the stairs and down the hallway. She noticed the paintings on the walls. The house was like a miniature museum.

"Dang, this place is like a mansion," she said.

"I guess it is a mansion, though I've never thought of it that way."

He opened the door to his father's office. The walls were decorated with plaques and awards for journalism. There were a number of framed war photographs. Javier proudly showed Akeelah the display.

"I guess it's obvious my father's a journalist. A foreign correspondent. That's what I wanna be." He walked to the bookcase behind his father's desk and picked up a book. "My dad's written three books. This one was a *New York Times* bestseller."

Akeelah noticed a picture of Javier with his father on a speedboat, their arms around each other, clowning for the camera. She swallowed with emotion as she looked at the two of them, so obviously happy to be together.

"Is your dad as goofy-funny as you are?" she said.

"Yeah. On his best days he's goofier and funnier." Javier turned to her and studied her face. "What's your father do, Akeelah?"

"My daddy?" She looked away, her mind racing, wondering how much to tell him. She had never confided in anyone, even Georgia, about the facts of her father's death.

"Uh…he used to work for the city parks."

Dropping the subject, she walked to the window and looked down at the birthday party below.

"Man, you got a lot of friends, Javier. I never had a birthday party half this big."

Javier took her hand and squeezed it. "Really? I'd think you'd have lots of friends." He stared into her eyes, then leaned forward and kissed her on the cheek.

Akeelah held her hand to her cheek and stared at him, caught in a swirl of emotions. "Why'd you do that?"

"I had an impulse," Javier said. He grinned. "Are you going to sue me for sexual harassment?"

Akeelah tried to keep a straight face as he fluttered his eyelashes at her, then she broke up laughing. Finally Javier was laughing, too, and the laughing fit lasted until tears were streaming from their eyes. She finally stopped laughing when she noticed something outside.

"Hey, what are they doin'?"

The kids were all gathered on the patio. Dylan was opening up several blue boxes.

"Oh, no," Javier said, rolling his eyes. "Dylan brought his Scrabble games. I hate to admit it, but he's a genius at Scrabble."

Akeelah looked at him with interest. "I really like Scrabble," she said.

They went into the backyard, where Dylan had poured out tiles next to each of the six rotating game boards on two picnic tables. He paced between the tables, his dark eyes serious beyond his years.

"I get thirty seconds for each board," he said. "That means each of you gets up to three minutes per turn."

His opponents were seated at five of the six boards. Dylan looked around. "We need one more. Who else wants to play?"

Akeelah stepped forward. "I will."

Dylan swung around to see Akeelah standing next to Javier. He forced a laugh. "Promise not to cry when I beat you?"

"I promise," she said, "if you promise."

Dylan abruptly stopped laughing and looked daggers at some of those who had found her comment funny. He gestured to the remaining game board and did a mock bow in Akeelah's direction. She nodded and sat down at her board.

"I'll keep score," Javier said. "We want to make sure this game's on the up-and-up."

He grabbed a pad of paper and a pen. Dylan's six opponents each pulled seven letters from their respective batches of tiles. Akeelah lined her letters up on her rack and studied them. She sensed Dylan's eyes boring into her, but did not look up.

In a sportscaster's voice, Javier said, "Hello, ladies and gentlemen, and welcome to the birthday party Scrabble extravaganza. I'm your host, Javier 'the Dude' Mendez, a k a the birthday boy. So let us now proceed…."

Dylan's first opponent, Roman, spelled out "birch."

"And right out of the gate, Roman scores thirty-two

84

points with 'birch' on the double-word score. Way to go, Roman!"

Javier scribbled down the score, while Dylan quickly built off Roman's "c" and spelled "crazy."

"But not to be outdone," Javier continued, "Dylan counters with an immediate use of the 'z' for thirty-eight big ones! The master is doing his usual magic." He flashed a look at Akeelah, wrinkling his nose.

She nodded and shuffled her letters around on her rack, while Dylan went up against Polly, who was seated next to her.

"Polly tests the water with 'acorn.' And the wily Dylan answers with a body blow—'beacon' for twenty! And now...a first-time player in our group—Akeelah Anderson." Everyone's eyes moved to Akeelah's board and watched as she quickly assembled "placebo," using all her letters. They all seemed stunned.

"Holy cannoli!" Javier yelled out. "A bingo right off the bat! Akeelah uses all her letters, getting fifty extra points, for a whopping...*eighty-two* big ones."

The partygoers murmured their approval. Dylan was not well liked and he had lorded it over the others for too long. They were eager to see someone bring him down to earth.

Dylan shook off his surprise at Akeelah's fast start and concentrated on his letters.

"What will Dylan do?" Javier said. "He's fighting the clock. You can cut the tension with a butter knife, folks."

Dylan looked up, his eyes bright with fury. "Shut up,

Mendez. How can anybody think with you babbling away?"

Javier made a face when Dylan turned back to the board. There was a tense moment as the clock ran down to the last seconds, and then Dylan smiled as he slowly spelled out the word "sharpens."

"Shazam!" Javier shouted. "Dylan gets his own bingo for seventy-six points. The old master coming up with new surprises."

Dylan stared at Akeelah with a smirk and she let out a long breath as she squinted at the board with fierce concentration. She couldn't believe he had countered her brilliant opening move so effectively, wiping out most of her advantage. She wasn't aware that Kiana and Georgia had come around the corner of the house and joined the other kids clustered around the picnic tables watching the games.

Dylan moved from board to board, making his moves quickly, almost disdainfully. One by one he eliminated the other players, building lopsided scores at each table. Polly, who was way behind, made a sudden comeback, enough to draw a frown from Dylan. But she, too, fell short.

Dylan now sat across from Akeelah (no longer standing, as he had at the other boards—a symbol of disdain for their abilities) at the only remaining Scrabble game. Twenty minutes of hard concentration had brought a sheen of sweat to his face.

"It's come down to this, folks," said Javier. "Having crushed all five other opponents, Dylan has only Akeelah to beat. But she's ahead by seventeen points with only a few letters left. Is this an upset in the making? Stay tuned. Don't you dare turn your dial…."

Georgia whispered to Kiana, "What kinda birthday party is this?"

"You got me," Kiana whispered back. "Why am I not surprised my sister's playin' Scrabble? That's all she ever does."

Dylan, fighting against time, spelled the word "lucid."

"Yowza!" Javier shouted. "Using the triple-word score, Dylan charges ahead by thirteen. This is a horse race, folks."

Akeelah chewed the inside of her cheek and tapped her foot on the ground. Her eyes were inches from the board as she analyzed the various possibilities. Dylan nervously glanced behind him to see his father standing with his arms crossed, looking none too pleased. Dylan smiled but there was no return smile from Mr. Watanabe.

Akeelah shuffled the letters on her rack as she continued to think.

"Just go," Dylan hissed.

She looked up to see him staring dead in her eyes, and she saw something in his expression that was unfamiliar. Not the old arrogance, the feeling that he was invincible. Was it fear? Was it possibly even respect?

She looked back at the board and spelled out the word "funnel."

"Hoo-*ya*," Javier exclaimed, bouncing on his feet with excitement. "Akeelah's back in the lead by seven and has two tiles left. But this could be Dylan's final play. What's he gonna do?"

Kiana, who understood the game but seldom played, smiled broadly at her sister's move. Mr. Watanabe continued to glower as his eyes roved over the board. Dylan, beads of sweat on his forehead, frowned at the board, muttering quietly under his breath. Then suddenly he smiled and looked up at Akeelah.

"*Arrivederci*, sweetheart," he said.

Using his three remaining tiles, he spelled "limn."

"Seven points ties the game," Javier said, some of his sportscaster's exuberance gone. "But Dylan gets Akeelah's last two points. He wins! A heartbreaker...."

Dylan walked off with his father, a tight grin on his face. Akeelah let out a long sigh as all the kids started chattering about the close match.

"Wow, Akeelah," Javier said, shaking her hand. "No one ever gets that close to beating Dylan. I'm really impressed."

"But I *didn't* beat him."

"Girl," Georgia said, "you passed up the mall to play *Scrabble?* You're loco and I'm never gonna figure you out. Forever trippin', that's you."

Akeelah gave her friend a wan smile but said nothing. She went inside the house and grabbed her purse from the hallway. As she was about to leave, she heard an angry voice in the living room and she stopped to listen. She tiptoed to the door and peeked around the corner and saw Mr. Watanabe pointing a finger at Dylan, his voice a low growl.

"If you can barely beat a little black girl at a silly board game, how do you expect to win the National Bee?"

Dylan bowed his head and said nothing. His father sharply struck the wall, causing both Dylan and Akeelah to jump.

"You listen to me," Mr. Watanabe said, his voice thick and threatening. "We're not coming in second again this year. Second is unacceptable. We are going to win, is that understood?"

Dylan nodded.

"You have to work a little harder."

"I don't think I can work any harder," Dylan said, his voice small, almost childlike.

"Yes, you can. You can always go the extra mile. And that's what you're going to do. Don't ever forget: you're my son."

"I know that."

Akeelah watched Mr. Watanabe lead his humiliated son out of the house.

Eight

Early Monday morning, Akeelah sat in a chair beside Dr. Larabee's desk, cradling an enormous book in her thin arms and reading aloud as he sat imperiously behind his desk, listening intently.

Akeelah read, "'He began to have a dim feeling that, to attain his place in the world, he must be himself, and not another.'" The book slipped from her fingers and fell to the floor. "Dr. Larabee, this book is *heavy*. My arms are beginning to hurt."

"Good," Dr. Larabee said. "You need to develop your arm muscles."

"I thought we were developin' my vocabulary."

"We are. But you have to remember, the mind and body are connected. Do you do any physical exercise?"

She smiled. "As little as possible. The school makes us take gym, but you can slide out of it if you want to. Crenshaw doesn't have many rules you can't break."

"You should build up your body," Dr. Larabee said.

"Should I lift weights?" she asked jokingly.

"Not a bad idea," he said seriously. "Keep reading."

"But I already *know* most of the words in this speech."

"It's not a speech," Dr. Larabee explained. "It's an essay by W. E. B. DuBois, the first black man to get a

Ph.D. from Harvard. He empowered blacks to be all that they could be. Unlike Booker T. Washington, who accommodated himself to the white culture—peace at any price—DuBois believed that blacks needed to be active politically, culturally, and intellectually. He was one of the great figures in African-American history."

"I know he was important and all," Akeelah said. "But shouldn't I be learning more big words? Isn't that what we're supposed to be doing?"

He looked at her sharply. "Are you questioning my teaching methods?"

She shook her head. "I'd never do that, Dr. Larabee."

Suddenly he broke into a smile, a rare event. "Well, maybe you should. I'm not infallible, and I do believe that DuBois would approve. But I *am* your teacher and, for better or worse, we'll do it my way." Just as suddenly, his old irritability had returned. "Spell 'cabalistic.'"

She tapped lightly on her thigh. "C-a-b-a-l-i-s-t-i-c."

Dr. Larabee took note of the way her hand tapped in rhythm with the letters. He had noticed this habit of hers before, and he sensed that it was something they should discuss because it might prove to be a useful strategy, but he didn't think the proper moment had arrived. He would bide his time and continue to monitor how she used her hand and how it affected her success with the most difficult words.

"And when did you learn 'cabalistic'?" he said.

"About two minutes ago, in this book. But in the time it took me to learn that one word, I'll bet Dylan probably learned *twenty*."

"You might be right, but that's beside the point."

"Why is it beside the point? It seems to *be* the point."

Dr. Larabee pointed a finger at her. "Don't get smart with me."

"I'm sorry."

"I'll tell you why it's beside the point. Dylan Watanabe may learn a hundred words to your one, but he's just a little robot. Wind him up and watch him spell. The people we're studying—DuBois, Dr. King, JFK—they used words to change the world. And they didn't acquire their vocabulary merely through rote memorization. The rote method will always trip you up in the end."

"Okay," Akeelah said, "but when I'm at the bee and they ask me to spell some little fish from Australia or some weird bacteria on the moon, I'm gonna wish we'd done a little more rote memorizing and not so much essay reading." She paused, realizing that she was criticizing his methods again, a definite no-no with this proud and brilliant man. "If you don't mind me saying."

There was an uncomfortable silence. Then Dr. Larabee said, "Bacteria don't exist on the moon."

"They don't?"

"No. The terrain is totally barren. Let me ask you something. "Where do you think 'big words' come from?"

"People with big brains?" she said.

He glowered at her for a moment, wondering if she was slyly poking fun at him, which she sometimes did. He then went to a huge tablet on an easel. He lifted up the cover, revealing a long handwritten list of difficult words.

"What do you see?" he asked.

"A bunch of big words that I don't know." She couldn't help adding, "And I *should* know."

"Look closer," he insisted. "What do you *see?*"

He covered part of the first word, "soliterraneous," so that only the first syllable, "sol," was showing.

"What kind of power do we get from the sun?" he continued.

"Solar power."

"So what's 'sol'?"

"Sun?"

He nodded. He then covered up "soli," leaving "terraneous."

"And what does 'terraneous' sound like?"

"…Terrain?" she said.

He nodded. "Exactly—meaning 'the earth.' Soli…terraneous….It means the sun and earth working together. So where do big words come from?"

Akeelah hesitated. "Little words? Combinations of them?"

Again he nodded. "And how many little words do you know?"

"Tons of them," she said. "More than I can count."

"And there are tons more to learn." He excitedly started pulling dictionaries off his shelf. "Greek ones and Latin ones and French ones. If you learn them all, you can spell *any* word, no matter how seemingly big."

She looked at the daunting stack of books and shook her head.

"Uh, maybe we should go back to the essay reading."

"What's the matter?" Dr. Larabee said. "I thought you wanted to win the National Bee. Isn't that what you're doing here, putting up with what I'm sure you consider my bullying and cranky disposition?"

"Well, maybe just gettin' there this time is good enough."

He shook his head back and forth with angry emphasis. "Oh, come on, Akeelah, don't give me that baloney. You want to win so badly it keeps you up at night. You dream about it, obsess about it. Ever since you found out there was a National Bee, you've seen yourself holding up that trophy. Am I right?"

"I guess so."

"You *know* I'm right. But you can't *win* it if you can't *say* it. *So say it.* Don't hold back. Sing it out loud and clear."

"I wanna win."

"No, I can't hear you. I don't hear the conviction. Say it louder!"

"I wanna win." When she saw no reaction from Dr. Larabee, she flung up an arm, her hand in a fist, and yelled out, *"I wanna win the National Spelling Bee!"*

"Much better," Dr. Larabee said. "But you'll win using *my* methods. By first understanding the power of language—and then by deconstructing it. Breaking it down to its roots, its origin. You will consume it and you will own it. And then you know what you'll be?"

"Tired," she said with a sigh. "Very, very tired."

"No." He smiled. "You, Akeelah Anderson, will be a champion. So are you ready?"

She paused and then nodded.

"Then let's go," he said. "Our work has just begun."

*

During the next few weeks Akeelah worked harder than she had ever imagined possible. She furiously wrote down words, dictated by Dr. Larabee. He guided her through columns of prefixes and suffixes. He taught her to draw interconnecting lines between foreign roots and their English counterparts. She walked around his office reading aloud from Shakespeare while he listened and then discussed Shakespearean language with her, and then he walked around Akeelah, pumping her with words from flashcards. While she sat in his office memorizing words, Dr. Larabee dictated a list of words into a recorder. At night, in her bedroom, Akeelah wore headphones at her computer and typed the words from Dr. Larabee's dictation.

One morning she complained to him that she didn't feel she was getting anywhere. It was hot and they were sitting on the front porch as Dr. Larabee listened to Akeelah read from a book of Greek mythology. They had become quite comfortable with each other over time, and the old tensions and doubts between them had gradually resolved. Akeelah looked up from her reading and said, "There's this ocean of words and all it's gonna take is one li'l old word to trip me up. I'm discouraged, Dr.

Larabee. I'm also bone-tired and I've got a splitting headache."

He stared at her. "Do you want to quit?"

She sighed heavily. "Sometimes I think I should."

"I think you're feeling sorry for yourself."

"Maybe I am."

"Make up your mind what you're going to do, because I'm not going to waste my time."

"I don't want to quit, Dr. Larabee. I'm just feelin' low."

"That can happen. But when you feel you've reached the limit of your endurance, you know what you have to do?"

"What?"

"You have to push a little harder. This is brutal work. You didn't dream it would be this demanding, did you?"

"No."

He regarded her for a moment and then said, "I never compliment you, do I?"

She smiled. "If you did, I'd drop dead with shock."

"Would you like me to compliment you?"

"Honestly?"

He nodded.

"Well, I guess I would. But believe me, I'm not expectin' it."

"Maybe one day I will. But don't hold your breath. We have a long way to go before we can pat ourselves on the back."

She looked down at her book. "A long way to go," she

Akeelah (Keke Palmer) and Georgia (Sahara Garey) encounter Steve on their way home from school in South Los Angeles.

Devon (Lee Thompson Young) is home from the service for an Anderson family dinner prepared by his mother (Angela Bassett).

Principal Welch (Curtis Armstrong) and Akeelah's sister, Kiana (Erica Hubbard), cheer Akeelah on at the District Bee.

Keke Palmer as
Akeelah Anderson.

Laurence Fishburne as
Dr. Joshua Larabee.

An intense game of Scrabble commences between Akeelah (Keke Palmer) and Dylan (Sean Michael Afable). Real-life spelling bee champion George Hornedo plays Roman (seated, center).

Dylan (Sean Michael Afable) receives a stern lecture from his domineering father (Tzi Ma).

Dr. Larabee (Laurence Fishburne) agrees to become Akeelah's (Keke Palmer) spelling coach.

Dr. Larabee (Laurence Fishburne) coaches Akeelah (Keke Palmer) by introducing her to great works of literature.

Dr. Larabee (Laurence Fishburne) discovers Akeelah's mnemonic device, jumping rope.

ABOVE: Tanya (Angela Bassett) confronts Akeelah (Keke Palmer) at the Regional Bee while Mr. Welch (Curtis Armstrong) and Dr. Larabee (Laurence Fishburne) look on.

RIGHT: Tanya (Angela Bassett) forgives Akeelah (Keke Palmer) and begins to support her daughter's dream.

The winners of the Regional Bee display their ribbons. From left to right, Dylan (Sean Michael Afable), Javier (J. R. Villarreal), and Akeelah (Keke Palmer).

Akeelah (Keke Palmer) smiles for the cameras with Mr. Welch (Curtis Armstrong) after qualifying for the Scripps National Spelling Bee.

Tanya (Angela Bassett) tries to persuade Dr. Larabee (Laurence Fishburne) to continue coaching Akeelah.

Dr. Larabee (Laurence Fishburne) shows Akeelah (Keke Palmer) a bust of Frederick Douglass in Washington, D.C.

Akeelah (Keke Palmer) gives it her all at the Scripps National
Spelling Bee.

Kiana (Erica Hubbard) and Terrence (Julito McCullum) watch as
their sister makes history at the televised bee.

Dylan (Sean Michael Afable) and Akeelah (Keke Palmer) share the spelling bee title.

Tanya (Angela Bassett), Akeelah (Keke Palmer), Dr. Larabee (Laurence Fishburne), and Javier (J. R. Villarreal) all celebrate Akeelah's inspiring win.

Writer and director Doug Atchison discusses a scene with Keke Palmer and Angela Bassett.

said and nodded. "You know what I like the most about you?"

"I'm not sure I want to know."

"You never lie to me."

*

One early summer afternoon, Akeelah had just arrived home from Dr. Larabee's and was quietly reading aloud from a Latin textbook as she entered the house and headed toward her room.

"Akeelah?"

She turned with a start, hiding the book behind her. She saw a somber-looking Tanya smoking a cigarette at the kitchen table.

"What d'ya got there?" she said.

"Nothin', Ma. Homework. Why you home so early?"

"I wasn't feeling good. They let me off early."

Tanya's eyes were bloodshot, as though she had been crying. On the table were a number of old photo albums open to pictures of a younger Tanya with Akeelah's father.

"You know…? The Regional Spelling Bee's coming up very soon," Akeelah ventured.

"Is that one gonna be in Beverly Hills, too?" Her mother sighed and kneaded her forehead with her thumb and first finger. "I told you, once you pass summer school you can start worrying about spelling bees again."

"But—"

"Akeelah, I don't have time for this right now. You're always fighting me and I'm not in the mood for it."

Akeelah studied her mother, who looked gray with fatigue. "You okay, Ma?"

"Just a little under the weather."

Akeelah nodded and then disappeared into her bedroom. Tanya continued to sit at the table smoking her cigarette. She slowly shook her head and sighed. There was just nothing she could do with that child. She had never had control over Akeelah. The girl existed in an orbit all her own, spinning through space in her own way.

*

It took Akeelah three weeks to get up the nerve to ask Dr. Larabee anything resembling a personal question. She picked a moment when she thought he might be distracted. He was pulling weeds from his flower garden, and she stood on the patio watching. A neighbor's dog was barking and soon was joined by a wailing chorus of other dogs.

"I was wondering something," Akeelah said. "Teaching comes so naturally to you. So how come you don't teach anymore?"

"I do teach," he said, without looking up. "I told you. Online."

"But isn't that kinda boring, sitting in front of the computer all day? No kids to interact with."

"I've got you, Akeelah. That's enough."

"I think I'd go crazy if I didn't have a change of scenery. Start to talk to myself, not that I don't do that already."

"When I want a change of scenery, I come out here."

"It seems so strange to me—having students and never getting to really see them."

"That's all right. Most of them aren't...as committed as you."

Akeelah smiled. That was the first compliment she had ever received from Dr. Larabee and she cherished it. She realized how much she craved his good opinion, and she was beginning to wonder if she was doing the National Bee as much for him as for herself, to fulfill something in him that she sensed he needed.

"No more dawdling," he said. "Let's keep going. Spell 'effervescent.'"

The sound of the dogs barking rent the air. Akeelah gritted her teeth. She wondered if they had barking dogs in Woodland Hills. Somehow she was certain the dogs out there were better behaved.

"...e-r-v-e..."

Dr. Larabee watched Akeelah's customarily tapping hand as it wavered and paused on her thigh.

"Uh...s-e-n-t..."

"Oh, come on. You know the word."

"The dogs are distracting me."

"Don't blame the dogs. When you get to the National Bee, you'll have bigger distractions than a bunch of canines howling at the moon."

He decided that the moment had come to delve into her mysterious habit. "What's that you do with your hand? I've noticed it since the first time you spelled for me."

"What?"

"Your hand. When you spell a word you go"—he began rhythmically tapping his thigh—"like that. Are you keeping count?"

"I don't know," she said, confused. "I don't really know I'm doing it."

He looked thoughtful.

"Come with me," he said.

She followed him to the back of the garden, where he pulled a large dusty cardboard box out from a shelf where he kept a vast array of tools. He gently lowered it onto the hood of his car. Akeelah watched him open the lid to reveal a cache of old toys. She felt she might have exhausted her luck by asking him some personal questions earlier, but she couldn't help herself. A question burned in her and she had to risk asking it.

"What do you got all those toys for?"

"Let's rephrase the question. 'What do you *have* all those toys for?' They used to belong to my…niece."

"Oh." She felt that he wasn't telling the truth, or not all of the truth. "So—you got any kids of your own?"

He looked at her, mildly irritated. "You ask a lot of questions, don't you?"

"I'm naturally inquisitive."

"That's often confused with being naturally obnoxious. You shouldn't pry so much." He found what he was looking for in the box. "Ah, here we go." He pulled out an old jump rope.

After he folded it neatly in his hand, they returned to the patio and he handed it to her.

"Okay," he said, "let me see you jump rope."

She looked at the rope and then at him. "Just jump?"

"Yes, jump."

She started to skip rope and, as Dr. Larabee watched her closely, she felt a sudden surge of joy and a wave of remembrance. Until the age of nine she had skipped rope with Georgia for hours at a time, and then for some reason she had given it up. She wasn't even sure she had a jump rope anymore. Maybe she would look for it when she got home. She was soon breathing hard (*I don't remember ever being out of breath when I was nine,* she thought) and stopped jumping.

"Is there a point to this?" she said.

He was clearly flustered and she couldn't figure out why. He was a man of many moods, but being flustered was one that she hadn't seen before. She was dying to ask him what was wrong, but she felt she had used up her quota of questions for the day.

"Yes, there's a point to it," he said. "Keep going."

"I'm a little out of shape."

"You're an eleven-year-old girl. That's very sad," he said, but he didn't sound sympathetic. "Keep going."

She kept jumping and Dr. Larabee picked up the lid of a metal trashcan and started banging loudly on it. Again Akeelah stopped, sucking air.

"I said keep going! Stay focused. I want you to spell 'effervescent' and don't think about anything else."

As Akeelah kept jumping, she said, "E-f-f..."

Dr. Larabee picked up two trashcan lids and moved closer to her, banging on them like cymbals. Akeelah kept her eyes focused straight ahead, spelling the word in time to her jumps.

"e-r-v..."

He moved right next to her, ratcheting up the noise. "...e-s-*c*-e-n-t."

Dr. Larabee stopped banging and gave her the strangest look. Akeelah stopped jumping and grinned at him.

"You see that?" he said excitedly. "That's your trick. Your mnemonic device."

"Jumping rope?"

"Keeping time," he told her. "You see kids at the bee doing all kinds of crazy things, looking for the edge. Some of them sway back and forth. Others turn in circles. They do whatever it takes to stay focused. *You* keep time. And I'll bet that if you learned the words *while* you kept time, you'd remember them that much better." He gave her a knowing grin. "I think maybe we've unlocked the puzzle of Akeelah Anderson. Now we have something new to practice, and I guarantee you that if you don't win the bee, at least you're going to be in great physical shape."

"Oh boy," she said. "I didn't expect this. You're full of surprises, Dr. Larabee."

"Let's start," he said. "You ready?"

"As ready as I'm ever gonna be."

Akeelah started jumping rope as Dr. Larabee shot her words from index cards, deliberately picking the most difficult ones. Later, he turned a long rope tied to a tree as Akeelah skipped and spelled. She skipped rope down the sidewalk as Dr. Larabee walked beside her, feeding her words. Against the setting sun, Akeelah kept jumping as Dr. Larabee gave her words while he sat at a picnic table.

"I'm gonna be doing this in my sleep."

"I hope so," he said. "Jump and spell. Jump and spell. We've had a big breakthrough today."

Nine

The enormous sign said: SOUTHERN CALIFORNIA REGIONAL SPELLING BEE, emblazoned in bright red. Scores of middle-schoolers gathered outside the auditorium with their nervous parents. Akeelah, Mr. Welch, and Dr. Larabee had just arrived and were standing in the crush of people, waiting for the doors to open so that Akeelah could register and pick up her ID.

"It's too bad your mother couldn't be here today, Akeelah," Mr. Welch said.

"Well, she wanted to come but she works on Saturdays." She was craning her neck, looking for friends. Suddenly she shouted, "Hey, there's Javier." She rushed over to Javier, who was standing with Polly and Roman. He gave her a huge grin and a playful hug, doing a little dance step with her.

A few minutes later they went inside and the Regional Judge, a perky professor wearing a dark suit and a pink blouse in startling contrast, addressed the audience. About a hundred spellers were seated on the stage behind her. Three other Judges and a Pronouncer sat facing the stage.

"Thank you for coming to USC for the Southern California Regional Spelling Bee," said the Regional Judge with a pretty smile. "It's very exciting for all of us.

We'll be giving out trophies to our top three spellers, who will represent Southern California at the National Spelling Bee in Washington."

The faces of the eager spellers were following her every word. They knew this was their chance—maybe the only chance they would ever have—to follow the glory all the way to Washington, D.C. Akeelah was twitching in her seat, brimming with nervous excitement.

Mr. Welch and Dr. Larabee were sitting close to the stage, Dr. Larabee as calm as Mr. Welch was nervous.

"So what do you think, Josh?" said the principal. "Does she stand a chance?"

Dr. Larabee took a long time to answer. "We'll see," he said finally, not the reassurance Mr. Welch was looking for. "She has the gift. But does she have the character to go with it? Time will determine that."

Ten minutes later Akeelah approached the mike. She seemed calm and her hand was already tapping lightly on her upper thigh. She's preparing herself, Dr. Larabee thought. Getting the rhythm down, almost like a jazz musician.

"A-l-f-r-e-s-c-o," Akeelah said. "'Alfresco.'"

Mr. Welch joined the applause. Dr. Larabee clapped twice and then put his hands on his knees. Mr. Welch sneaked a look at his friend, who showed no expression.

"Not such a hard word," Mr. Welch said. He laughed. "If I can spell it, it's not a hard word."

Dr. Larabee shook his head. "Believe me, they're all hard when you're onstage in front of hundreds of people."

Mr. Welch fell into silence, chastened by his friend's implied criticism.

The spellers started dropping like flies.

"...t-i-o-u-s," said a skinny speller. "'Loquacious.'"

Ding went the bell.

"E-s-p-a-d-r-i-l-e," a tall speller said.

Ding.

"S-c-o-p-a-l-a-m-i-n-e," a cross-eyed speller said, looking at the Pronouncer with longing in his eyes, hoping that somehow he might have spelled it right.

Ding.

Twenty minutes later, Polly was at the mike for her second round. Only about a quarter of the spellers were left onstage.

"'Malloseismic,'" said the Pronouncer.

Polly looked confused and rubbed her hands together nervously. "Could you repeat the word, please?"

"Malloseismic."

Polly nodded. Slowly she said, "M-a-l-o-s-e-i-s-m-i-c."

Ding.

Polly walked down to her parents, who comforted her as she started to cry into her mother's blouse. Her father held her hand and kissed her on the cheek.

Good parents, Akeelah thought. *Polly is very lucky.* She looked worriedly at Javier, who shrugged his shoulders as if to say, "Them's the breaks. What you gonna do?"

Another twenty minutes passed and now there were only a handful of contestants left, including Dylan, Javier, and an increasingly confident Akeelah. Javier took the mike and grinned at the audience, always ready to play the clown.

"The word is 'doublure,'" said the Pronouncer.

As Javier was thinking, the rear entrance to the auditorium opened and a very unhappy Tanya Anderson entered the room. When Mr. Welch caught sight of her, he motioned with his hand for her to join him. He pointed to an empty seat on his left. She shook her head no and glared at the stage. Mr. Welch leaned over and whispered to Dr. Larabee, "I think there's some trouble ahead."

Akeelah, who had not yet spotted her mother, smiled at Javier as he returned to his seat. "Nice job, Javier. 'Doublure' is kinda tough."

"Luckily I knew the word."

Now it was Akeelah's turn to take the mike.

"Your word is 'psalmody,'" he said.

Akeelah frowned. "Definition, please?"

"The practice or art of singing psalms. 'Psalmody.'"

There was a commotion in the back of the auditorium. Akeelah squinted in the bright lights, trying to see what was going on.

"Do you need him to repeat the word?" the Judge asked.

"No," Akeelah said. "'Psalmody.' P-s-a—"

"Without my permission!" The sound of her mother's voice sliced right through Akeelah's brain.

Voice trembling, she said, "Uh…l-m-o…"

Mr. Welch had rushed to the back of the auditorium and was trying to calm Tanya down. People, including the Judges, strained to see what was happening. Some even stood.

"…d-y," Akeelah said faintly. "'Psalmody.'"

She quickly returned to her seat and kept her head down. She was too confused and disheartened to respond to Javier's thumbs-up. It was all she could do to fight back a flood of tears.

The Judge looked hard at Akeelah and then at the ruckus in the back of the auditorium. "Um, okay…. Next contestant."

Dylan took the mike. Akeelah glanced up and saw a very frustrated Mr. Welch coming down to the stage. He gestured to her urgently, but she ignored him. He turned to the Judge.

His voice cracking with embarrassment, he said, "Excuse me, I'm sorry. One of the speller's mothers needs to speak with her. I'm afraid it's rather urgent."

The Judge nodded and regarded Mr. Welch coolly. "This is irregular."

"I understand that."

"Well, if she's not back onstage by her next turn, she's disqualified."

"Oh, she'll be back. This will just take a minute."

He frantically gestured to Akeelah, who glanced over at the smirking Dylan. She then turned to Javier and he gave her an encouraging but wan smile. Humiliated, she got to her feet and slunk off the stage, her hands held stiffly to her sides. Javier followed her with his eyes, looking very concerned.

Tanya, Akeelah, and Mr. Welch stood just outside the

auditorium's rear door. Dr. Larabee followed them a moment later.

"Mrs. Anderson, I swear we thought you were onboard with this," Mr. Welch said.

Tanya turned on Akeelah, speaking through clenched lips. "You wanna tell me what's going on? I never signed any consent form. You've got some explaining to do, young lady."

Akeelah nervously looked at Dr. Larabee, who seemed as perplexed as Mr. Welch. Then she looked down, ashamed. She wished she could shrivel into nothing. Disappear from this world forever.

"I signed Dad's name to it," she said finally, in a small voice.

"You did *what?*" Tanya said, her voice rising. She was so enraged she took a threatening step toward Akeelah, who shrank back.

"How do you think I felt when your friend Javier's mother called to see if I needed a ride to USC? I didn't know what she was talking about, or who she was. I felt like a fool."

"I'm sorry, Mama. I just wanted to do the bee. I had my heart set on it."

"And you were willing to do it by lying to me? Going behind my back all this time? How can I ever trust you again?" She let out a breath of sadness, anger, and disappointment. "Say goodbye to your friends, Akeelah, 'cause this is your last spelling bee. You are grounded."

She grabbed Akeelah by the hand to leave, but Mr. Welch intervened.

"Mrs. Anderson, I *beg* you to reconsider. Akeelah's doing this as much for Crenshaw as for herself. If she wins, there's so much we'll be able to accomplish for the school. New textbooks, needed repairs, some important hirings." He turned to Dr. Larabee. "Josh, please...tell Mrs. Anderson how you've been working with Akeelah and how gifted she is. She *deserves* this opportunity."

Dr. Larabee stood there, trying to make sense of what was happening. He looked into Akeelah's desperate eyes and then felt the heat of Tanya's anger and sense of betrayal. He had a decision to make and it was not going to be an easy one.

"No," Dr. Larabee said, shaking his head. "Mrs. Anderson's right. Akeelah doesn't deserve to go to the bee this year. She lied to her mother and that's unforgivable."

"What?" Mr. Welch stared at his friend, openmouthed. "I can't believe what I'm hearing. Yes, Akeelah made a mistake, but doesn't she deserve a second chance?"

"Dr. Larabee," Akeelah said. "Please...."

He turned to her and said solemnly, "You have to learn to respect your mother's wishes." He then trained his gaze on Tanya, and after a pause said, "I apologize if we contributed to any anguish you're feeling, Mrs. Anderson."

Tanya took a moment to size up this tall, dignified stranger before responding. "Who are you exactly, sir?"

"My name's Joshua Larabee, ma'am. And I've been helping Akeelah prepare for the spelling bee."

"You mean while she was supposed to be going to summer school?"

"I'd been told that our lessons were taking the place of summer school. It seems that I was misinformed."

Mr. Welch chimed in, saying, "No, you weren't. Mrs. Anderson—Akeelah has earned school credit studying with Dr. Larabee. We worked out a special program just for her."

Tanya grabbed Akeelah's arm. "Why didn't you tell me about that?"

"I didn't think you'd let me do it." She wiped her eyes and blew her nose. "Mama, I hated goin' behind your back. It bothered me every single day. But every time I brought up the bee, you didn't wanna hear it. I didn't know what to do." She reached out and touched her mother's hand, looking deeply remorseful. "I'm sorry, Mama."

The four fell into a tense silence, broken by Dr. Larabee, who said, "Mrs. Anderson...Akeelah's clearly forfeited her opportunity to participate in the bee this year. But if I may.... Your daughter has a remarkable gift. She's able to process and retain information as well as anyone I've ever known. So at the very least, I hope that you would consider letting her do the bee...next year. I really believe that a gift like hers shouldn't be wasted."

Tanya stared at Dr. Larabee for a long moment and then turned to Akeelah, who still looked chagrined.

At the same time they were debating Akeelah's fate outside the auditorium door, another speller left the stage in bitter disappointment and Javier stared nervously at the rear of the auditorium for a glimpse of Akeelah. She was taking too much time. It was his turn to spell, with Akeelah to follow. When his number was called, he pretended not to hear.

"Number seventy-two, let's go," the Judge said sharply.

In an effort to buy time any way he could, Javier walked very slowly to the mike. He then bent over and retied one of his shoelaces. The Judges observed his slow-down with a mixture of confusion and annoyance.

Tanya was now wrestling with what to do. She was impressed by Dr. Larabee and at the same time still very angry at Akeelah. She felt betrayed and it hurt. It wouldn't be easy to rebuild the trust she felt she had always had with her youngest child. She turned back to Dr. Larabee.

"Dr. Larabee. You are a doctor, aren't you?"

"A professor of English, yes."

"Do you think Akeelah actually has a chance at winning the National Spelling Bee?"

"Well, she has to get through the Regionals first. But yes, I think she has a good chance."

Tanya nodded, not taking her eyes off him.

"Mama, I'm so sorry for what I did."

Tanya slowly turned to her. "You never lied to me before in your life. I'm pretty sure of that. You must want this thing pretty bad."

"'Pretty bad' doesn't describe it."

"Well, then, maybe you can tell me what you think a good punishment would be for what you did?"

Akeelah looked at Dr. Larabee.

"Your mother asked you a question," he said.

Akeelah reluctantly turned to her mother, and said with difficulty, "I guess I gotta miss the bee."

After a moment's hesitation, Tanya said, "Well, that doesn't just punish you. Mr. Welch and Dr. Larabee put a lot of time into this, too. So think of something else."

A glint of hope glowed in Akeelah's eyes, and Mr. Welch's expression was trained on Tanya as though through the intensity of his gaze, he could will her into acquiescence.

"Uh…maybe double chores for the next month?"

Tanya shook her head. "Try *three* months." She turned to Mr. Welch. "Does she still have time to get back onstage?"

"If we move quickly."

Tanya squeezed her daughter's shoulder. "Then you better get movin'."

"C'mon, Akeelah," Mr. Welch said, "we don't have much time."

Dr. Larabee nodded. "The Judges are not very forgiving about infractions."

Akeelah looked at her mother, leaned forward, and kissed her cheek. "Thank you, Mama," she said, and rushed into the auditorium with Mr. Welch.

Onstage, Javier was doing his antic best to stall for time.

"Can I get the pronunciation again?" he said.

"He's given it to you five times now," the Judge said, clearly running out of patience.

Javier tapped his hearing aid. "Hello? Is this thing

113

working? Mom," he called out to the audience, "did you bring my spare battery?" There was a wave of nervous laughter in the audience.

When Javier saw Akeelah and Mr. Welch rushing down the aisle, he said, "Ah, never mind. 'Ratatouille.' R-a-t-a-t-o-u-i-l-l-e."

He winked at Akeelah and strolled to his chair, leaving the Judges dazed and confused.

"Okay, where's Number seventy-three?" the Judge said. "I'm afraid she's going to have to be—"

"She's right here," Mr. Welch yelled out. He ushered Akeelah back onstage. Dylan, watching closely, shook his head and frowned. As Akeelah walked past Javier, he whispered, "Where *were* you? I was about to start tap dancing, and if that didn't work I planned to faint."

"Thanks, Javier," she whispered, and stepped up to the mike.

"The word is 'pluviosity,'" said the Pronouncer.

Tanya entered the auditorium and stood in the back, watching her daughter onstage, a whisper of a proud smile on her lips.

"Can I get a definition?" Akeelah said.

"'A state characterized by much rain; a condition of being rainy.'"

Akeelah took a deep breath and looked out at her mother watching her closely. She smiled and then said, "'Pluviosity.' P-l-u-v-i-o-s-i-t-y."

Tanya, her face suffused with amazement and pride, applauded heartily as her daughter took her seat.

Finally the contest was reduced to the three who

would go to Washington, D.C., for the National Bee: Dylan took first place, Javier second, and Akeelah third. Photographers snapped pictures of the three finalists. Flashbulbs burst and the three were interviewed.

Akeelah said, "I've got so many people to thank for this chance to win the National Bee, I don't know where to start. But there's my teacher, Ms. Cross, who got me to enter my school bee. Then there's Mr. Welch, my principal, standing over there. And a whole lot of other folks, friends and fellow students. And then there's Dr. Larabee, my spelling coach, and without him I wouldn't be here talkin' to you now. And there's my mother, Tanya Anderson, who's been so great. I love you, Ma...."

Ten

A huge blown-up newspaper photograph of the three finalists with the caption GOING TO THE NATIONAL BEE! was hanging over a pep rally in honor of Akeelah. The Crenshaw Middle School students cheered as the band played. Akeelah, overwhelmed by the fanfare, stood to the side while Mr. Welch addressed the crowd.

"We at Crenshaw have a lot to be proud of today," he intoned. "Thank you all for coming to this pep rally to honor our very own Akeelah Anderson. When she goes on and wins the National Spelling Bee"—the cheers ratcheted up to roars—"Crenshaw Middle School will be on the map!" He turned to Akeelah and gave her a hug. "Now, why don't I let the star of the moment say a few words. Akeelah…"

She simply stood there, staring out at the sea of faces, almost in a state of shock. Was this really happening to her or was it all a dream? How was it possible that little Akeelah Anderson, the one-time school weirdo, bookworm, and social outcast, could now suddenly be the flavor of the month? If it was a dream, she never wanted to awaken.

She slowly stepped up to the mike at Mr. Welch's frantic urging while the applause rained down on her.

"Um…thanks," she said. "Thanks a lot."

She looked over at Mr. Welch, not sure what else to say. He rushed back to the mike.

"What do you think about your chances in D.C., Akeelah?"

"Well…it's gonna be hard. 'Cause a lotta the other kids come from schools with Latin classes and stuff. One school I know of even teaches Greek." She smiled out at the audience. "Y'know, I've been buggin' Mr. Welch here for, like, a month to get a Latin class going at Crenshaw, but he said I need at least ten kids to sign up. So far I got only me and Georgia." She held up a pad of paper rolled up in her hand and waved it back and forth. "But maybe if y'all wanted to put your name on this list, we could get one!"

Her plea met with a resounding silence. Then Myrna yelled out, "Girl, you're trippin'. Ain't nobody wanna take no Latin."

Chuckie Johnson jumped up from his seat and said, "But we could use some new basketball courts. Ours really suck."

This suggestion was greeted with much laughter and whistles and Mr. Welch quickly returned to the mike.

"Tell you what," he said. "I'm going to make a promise right now and you can hold me to it. If Akeelah wins the National Bee, we'll find a way to get a Latin class *and* some new basketball courts."

Everybody broke into cheers.

At the end of the rally, Georgia pushed her way through a crowd of students gathered around Akeelah waiting to get her autograph.

"Girl, you're like a movie star now. How does it feel? It must be kinda wild."

"It's pretty freaky."

"Hey, my mama said she wants to take us out to celebrate tonight. You can pick the restaurant."

"Well, Javier's parents are taking me out. But maybe we can meet up later."

An excited Mr. Welch suddenly rushed up to Akeelah and grabbed her by the arm. "Listen, there's a reporter outside who wants to talk to you. She's from Channel 2. That's big time, Akeelah."

Sensing Georgia's discomfort, she shook her head decisively. "I don't wanna talk to no reporter."

"Are you kidding? This is the type of good publicity Crenshaw needs. This is your chance to really make a difference. Come on!"

He took Akeelah by the hand and led her away, leaving Georgia looking hurt and left out. She shook her head grimly and stalked out of the gymnasium.

A female reporter shook Akeelah's hand vigorously and began to interview her on-camera on the sidewalk outside Crenshaw.

"This is Jan Rafferty," she said to the camera, "reporting from South Los Angeles. I'm here with eleven-year-old Akeelah Anderson, a seventh-grader from Crenshaw Middle School who's heading to the Scripps National Spelling Bee. Akeelah, how does it feel to be going to Washington, D.C.?"

"Well, it's pretty cool," Akeelah said nervously. "I never thought it would happen to me."

"What do you think of your chances?"

Akeelah shrugged. "I try not to think about that. Hopin' won't win you any awards. I just got to keep workin', learnin' new words. That's the best way. Then if you fail, well, at least you gave it your best shot."

"Your parents must be proud of you."

Akeelah thought of her father and smiled for the first time.

"They are," she said.

While the interview was in progress, Dr. Larabee sat in his office with the lights off watching the broadcast. His expression was glum. He sipped a whiskey and muttered under his breath, "This is all nonsense. Just plain nonsense. The vultures are gathering around her."

He turned away from the screen and looked down at a photograph in his lap. In it, he was several years younger, much thinner, and was holding a young girl who looked to be about eight. They were both smiling. Dr. Larabee's eyes filled with sadness. He looked back at Akeelah's image on TV. She was saying, "While I'm in Washington I want to see the White House and the Senate and House of Representatives. And maybe the Supreme Court, too. All three branches of government. That would be cool...." Shaking his head, he turned off the television and put the photograph in a drawer, which he slammed shut.

He took a long sip of his drink and sat in the dark trying to stifle his emotions.

*

Two days later, a perplexed Akeelah stood before an unusually testy Dr. Larabee. She couldn't understand what was wrong. He had become so much warmer and approachable over the course of the summer, but today he seemed like a stranger.

"Did you see my TV interview?" she said.

"I'd rather not talk about it."

"Oh. Okay. I just thought you might have seen it."

He gave her a grim look. "Spell 'affenpinscher,'" he said.

"'Affen'—what?"

"'Grallatorial,'" he said. "Spell it, please."

"G-r-a-l-a—"

"Wrong," he cut in. "'Jacquard.'"

"Dr. Larabee," Akeelah said. "What's going on?"

"Spell the word. 'Jacquard.'"

Visibly upset, Akeelah said, "J-a-q-u—"

"What about the 'c'? These are all words *missed* in last year's National Bee, and you can't spell any of them."

"'Cause we haven't studied 'em yet. You're not being fair."

He continued to glare at her. "Why did you cancel yesterday? Were you doing another interview? Flaunting yourself on TV? Over what? Let's face some facts here. Third place in a regional competition is no cause for celebration. I thought you wanted to win the Nationals."

"I do," she said. "More than anything. And I wasn't doing another interview. I was at the mall."

Dr. Larabee pounded a fist on his desk. *"The mall?* Doing what?"

120

"Well, sometimes I just wanna have a life, you know? A little time to myself." She paused. "Look, I wasn't dissing you, Dr. Larabee. I was Christmas shopping."

Dr. Larabee's expression grew even more stormy. "'Dissing'? I thought we only used words from the dictionary in here."

Akeelah returned his glare, then opened the dictionary on his desk and found an entry.

"'Dis,'" she said. "'Dissed.' 'Dissing.' To treat with disrespect or contempt. To find fault with." She slammed the dictionary shut. "New words get added to the dictionary every year."

Dr. Larabee's expression slowly turned from angry to thoughtful. "Point accepted. You've clearly done your homework—and that's what you need to continue to do."

"I know."

"You can have a life *after* the spelling bee. You know, I didn't make it to the National Bee until I was fourteen. I had no help, no training—and I was out by the third round. Now you have an opportunity to *win this thing*."

"But all we've done for all this time is study words, Dr. Larabee. Why can't we take a break? Go see a movie or a game? Why can't we have fun for a change?"

"I told you, Denise, you can have fun after the bee."

Akeelah stared at him, looking confused. "Who's Denise?"

"What?"

"You called me Denise."

121

Now Dr. Larabee looked rattled. He started to speak but then shook his head and remained silent.

"Dr. Larabee…?"

He kept looking at her, seemingly sorting out something in his mind. Then he turned away and sat behind his desk with a heavy sigh.

"Are you okay?" Akeelah said.

He kept looking down and said finally, "Yes, I'm fine. I'm just fine." But to Akeelah he looked anything but fine.

He opened his desk drawer and pulled out several long, narrow boxes. He set them down on the desk in front of her.

"Here," he said. "I spent all last week making these for you."

"What are they?"

"Flashcards," he said. "For five thousand new words. The type of words you can expect at the Finals."

"Five *thousand?*" she said, and whistled. "But we're running out of time. What're you going to do, coach me twenty-four/seven?"

"No," he said, looking down at his desk. He paused before adding, "You can learn them on your own. I've taught you everything I can."

She approached the desk as his words slowly sank in. "What are you saying? You're not gonna work with me anymore?"

"You've got it all, Akeelah. Word construction. Etymology. Memorization techniques. There's nothing left to go over. You just need to focus on the words now. I'm putting it in your capable hands."

"But I can't learn five thousand new words by myself. No way!"

"Of course you can. You've got a brain like a sponge. Just sit down and study them."

"But I swear I won't miss any more sessions. And I'll do whatever you say. Please, Dr. Larabee, you can't stop coaching me now."

Dr. Larabee looked very distraught and couldn't make eye contact with her.

"You don't know your own power, Akeelah," he said. "You should read that quote again. You're afraid of your own strength. You have to accept your strength and go with it."

"I need you," she said. "I really do."

"Look—I told Mr. Welch I'd help you get through the Regionals. I did that. There's nothing left for me to offer you, Akeelah. Just learn these words and you'll do fine. All right?" He paused and then added, "You've already surpassed me."

Akeelah just stared at him, stupefied.

"I don't understand you," she said.

"That's not important."

"Okay," she said, "then that's it." Her eyes were moist and hot. She quickly gathered up the boxes of flashcards and stormed out, slamming the door shut behind her.

Dr. Larabee just sat there, staring at the closed door. He put his head in his hands and took a series of long, sighing breaths.

"I'm sorry," he muttered into his hands, "but it's gotten too tough. You're too close to me now and I can't have that. I called you Denise, and that's the trouble right there. You *aren't* Denise, you *aren't* my daughter, and you can never be. You can never be, Akeelah. You can never be…."

*

Akeelah sat in her bedroom that night, angry and upset. She stared at the boxes of flashcards on her desk. She didn't want to open them, had no urge to study for the first time in months. *What's the point?* she thought. *Without him I don't have a chance. Why doesn't he realize that? Why has he left me when we've worked so well together and we're so close to the final goal? Although I guess it's not "we," not anymore, and maybe it never was. He doesn't want it that way. He's left me on my own to fend for myself and I don't know why. I just don't have a clue. All I know is, I feel sick—sick inside….*

She took out a flashcard, read it, and then shoved it back in the box. She started to take out another, then shut the box, picked up the phone, and dialed. "Hey, girl. What up?" There was no response at the other end. "Georgia, you lost your tongue? It's Akeelah."

"Yeah," she said flatly. "I know who it is. I ain't forgot your voice."

"So whatcha doin'?"

"Watchin' TV. What I always do."

"You wanna go skating this weekend? I haven't used my blades in months."

Georgia paused before saying, "Why don't you go with your friends from Woodland Hills?"

"What? Girl, what's wrong with you? Why you sound all bent outta shape?"

"I'm fine." After a long, uncomfortable silence, she added, "You know somethin' I noticed about you?"

"What's that?"

"When you're with me and my friends, you talk one way—all down-home and stuff. But with your new friends you sound white, like them. Why is that? I can't help wonderin'."

Akeelah stared at the telephone receiver, unable to think of an answer.

"I got stuff to do," Georgia said. "I'll talk to you later." She abruptly hung up.

Akeelah shook her head, unable to believe this conversation with her oldest and best friend. First Dr. Larabee and now Georgia. She sensed that her safe existence was no longer safe. It was suddenly falling apart.

She sighed and started to open the box again when Kiana called from the living room. "Keelie, get in here. You're on TV!"

Akeelah walked slowly out of her room and joined her sister and mother, whose eyes were fastened to the TV.

"Look!" Kiana said.

On TV, Akeelah saw her own image on the news and for an instant she felt weirdly divided between two Akeelahs—the public one and the private one. Which one was she really?

The reporter on TV said, "Akeelah Anderson's ascension to the National Spelling Bee has captivated her community. All over South Los Angeles, people are talking about her—this eleven-year-old girl from Crenshaw Middle School who never entered a spelling bee till this year. She has quickly become an inspiration for her community, a beacon of hope for many."

She stuck the mike in front of Steve, who was hanging out, as usual, in front of the neighborhood liquor store, very shaky but offering the reporter a sweet, toothless smile.

"What do you think of this young girl, sir?"

"I know her, a good li'l girl. And she, ah, the whole thing...uh...it's good for all of us. You could say not too many good things happen around here." The top of a half-pint bottle of whiskey was sticking out of his pants pocket. "Let's hope she go all the way."

The scene shifted to an old woman outside her home.

"If she wins," said the old woman, "it's gonna be like all of us wins. It's 'specially a wonderful thing for all African Americans."

A thug on a street corner hopped up and down with excitement. "Yo, dat girl's dope! She da best."

As each of these sentiments was expressed, Akeelah's expression grew darker and darker, like a terrible weight was being placed on her shoulders, a weight she couldn't hope to carry with any semblance of grace. Dr. Larabee was right: it was all a trap, a trap set for her. She was beginning to understand that fame might have pitfalls. It was a spiderweb to capture you and put you on display for others to view, not as a human being but as an object.

"Oh, no," she muttered as she turned and ran from the room.

Tanya looked up, confused by her daughter's behavior.

Eleven

Akeelah threw herself on the bed and let the tears come. They were tears that she had been holding inside since she left Dr. Larabee's house. She beat her fists on the bed and wept with true anguish. A few minutes later Tanya entered the room, sat on the edge of the bed, and began rubbing Akeelah's back. She didn't speak until Akeelah's sobbing subsided and she began to breathe more evenly.

"What's wrong, baby?" she said. "Everything is going so good for you."

"I don't wanna do the bee no more, Mama. I'm sick of the whole thing."

"Not do the bee? But I just don't understand. You have your heart set on it."

"*Did* have. Not anymore."

Tanya increased the pressure on Akeelah's back and waited for her to continue.

"'Cause it's making my brain hurt. It's drivin' me crazy. Dr. Larabee won't coach me no more and Georgia don't wanna hang with me. My world's fallin' apart, Mama. And all those people, people in the streets, they're *expectin'* me to win—and if I don't win, what then? It's just too hard. I want it all to stop."

"But baby—"

"Please, Mama. Try to understand what I'm tellin' you." Akeelah hugged her mother and began to sob again. Tanya held her, rocked her, and looked very worried. She made a decision. She would go to Dr. Larabee's house and confront him. He must have some answers for her. *Somebody* had to have some answers, and she would dig and dig until she found them.

Dr. Larabee answered the buzzer immediately, as though he had been expecting a visitor. His expression was mildly friendly but she could tell he was surprised to see her.

"Come in my office," he said. "Would you like coffee? I have some made."

"No, thank you."

"I'm having a whiskey. Could I offer you that?"

"I don't drink." She sat down and plunged right in to the concerns that had sent her out of the house late at night. "I'm worried about Akeelah," she said. "She's talking about quitting the bee."

"That's her decision to make, Mrs. Anderson. Akeelah is a very strong-willed girl. She's going to do what she wants to do."

"But that's *not* what she wants to do. I know my daughter. Right now she's just very, very upset." She paused and then added, "Mainly upset with you. She says you won't go on working with her."

Dr. Larabee sipped his drink as he stared at Tanya. "Well, I certainly didn't mean to upset the girl. I actually thought I was doing the best thing for her."

"How can abandoning her be the best thing for her? I don't understand that."

129

Dr. Larabee shook his head and leaned forward. "I'm not abandoning her. That's absolutely not the case. I've given her all the tools she needs to succeed. And if I may say so, Mrs. Anderson, I was supportive of Akeelah's spelling endeavors long before many others were."

Tanya nodded, absorbing his veiled criticism. "I know you were, Dr. Larabee, and I appreciate that. I was too busy earnin' a living to pay much attention. And that was wrong, I realize that now. And I want to make amends any way I can."

Dr. Larabee nodded. "I appreciate your candor."

Drawing in a deep breath, Tanya said, "You know, Dr. Larabee, Akeelah is only eleven. She seems much older in many ways, but that's because she's so bright. She's already been through so much in her life. Her father was killed three years ago. It was a drive-by shooting when he went out to buy a pack of cigarettes." She grimaced and tried to smile. "That's the kind of neighborhood we live in."

"I live in the same neighborhood."

"Then you can understand. Do you have any idea what it's like for a young girl to lose a father that way?"

He slowly nodded as his eyes slid away from her. "I can imagine."

"Well, then, why do you want to cause this child any more grief? Hasn't she had enough?"

"I feel you're accusing me, Mrs. Anderson, and that's unfair." Suddenly Dr. Larabee, so articulate, was struggling for words. "And I've told you...I've tried to make it clear that I'm just not in a place where I can be of much help to Akeelah right now."

"But she needs you."

"How do you know that?"

"I just know. Call it a mother's intuition."

"Well, I beg to differ, Mrs. Anderson. It's not me who Akeelah needs."

He looked her straight in the eye. Tanya stared back, fire in her eyes, then angrily got up and stalked out of the house.

*

Akeelah, watching TV in the living room, looked up expectantly when Tanya returned home.

"What'd he say?"

Tanya expelled a deep breath. "He's just not feeling good, Akeelah. If you want my opinion, something is eating at that man. Something deep. And he's having a whole lot of trouble dealin' with it."

Akeelah looked down, fighting to control her emotions. "He just doesn't think I can win and he's backin' away."

"No, that's not true. I'm good at readin' people, and Dr. Larabee is a good man. But he's hurting inside. You don't see it because you've got your own concerns." Tanya turned off the television and sat next to Akeelah, holding her hand.

"Listen, I wanna tell you something. You know why I didn't want you to do the bee at first? 'Cause I watched that video of yours. And I saw one winner and two hun-

dred losers. I didn't want you to be one of those losers."
She pinched Akeelah's cheek, forcing a smile from her.
"But when I saw you on that stage, I realized you'd
already won. Just by goin' for your dream, you won.
Anything more would be gravy." She studied Akeelah's
face, but there was no reaction. "Did I ever tell you I went
to college right after high school?"

"No," Akeelah said, looking at her mother with interest. "You never mentioned it."

"Well, I did. I had a scholarship to USC. My ambi-
tion was to be a doctor. But I felt completely out of place
at that school. And I convinced myself I was gonna fail.
So before that could happen, I dropped out. I felt I was
protecting myself from failing, but I was setting my own
self up for failure." She ran her hand through Akeelah's
hair and said softly, "I don't want you doin' the same
thing with this bee."

"I don't wanna drop out, Mama. But I need Dr.
Larabee, I really do. I can't see doing this without him."

Tanya studied her daughter carefully.

"You're very fond of that man, aren't you?"

"I don't know."

"I think you know."

"Well, I do respect him a lot. He can be grumpy and
difficult…and yet…well, there's something about him—
he's really kind underneath and he's so smart."

Tanya said softly, "Your father was kind and he was
very smart."

"What are you sayin'?"

"He reminds you of your father, right? Doesn't he remind you of your father?"

"Yeah, in some ways." She added bitterly, "But not right now, he doesn't."

Tanya opened one of the boxes sitting on the table in front of the TV, carefully removed a card, and studied it. "I'm just gonna have to play Dr. Larabee," she said. "'Gabbro.' A group of dark, heavy rocks. 'Gabbro.'" She looked up. "Can you spell it?"

"G-a-b-r-o," Akeelah said.

"Actually, there's two 'b's.'"

Akeelah nodded and sighed. "I guess I'm just not in the mood right now."

Tanya said, "Y'know, you're not short on people who'd wanna help you, Akeelah. This is what fame is like—even a little bit of fame. You don't know these people, but these people know you. They've read about you, they've seen you on TV. And believe me, they're pullin' for you. Look around you: there's probably fifty thousand folks who'd like to coach you. Starting with me."

Akeelah smiled and gripped her mother's hand. "Mama...you ever think you might go back to college? How cool would that be?"

Tanya looked into her daughter's eyes for a long moment. "I just might," she said. She pulled out another card. "'Cedilla....'"

*

The next day, in a much brighter mood, Akeelah went outside with one of her boxes to study words. Suddenly Terrence appeared beside her.

"Yo," he said.

Akeelah stopped and turned to him. "Hey, Terrence, you on your way to summer school?"

"Maybe, maybe not. For me to know and you to find out."

"You better stop skippin' school, boy. They're gonna hold you back."

"Not for the first time." He gave a wry grin. "Pretty soon you're gonna pass me and graduate first."

"That's not true," she said. "You're smart. You can do whatever you want to do."

"You one of them motivational people now?"

"Only with you, big brother."

Akeelah always tried to be gentle with Terrence because she knew his history, especially his early academic woes. He had taken his father's death very hard. When Terrence was ten he was diagnosed as dyslexic (no one in the school system had ever suggested that his language problems were a direct result of dyslexia). During the last year of Mr. Anderson's life, he had worked with Terrence on a daily basis. Terrence had begun to flower under his father's tutelage, and then suddenly his father was taken away. From that day on, Terrence grew colder and more inward. He began skipping school and hanging out with the wrong crowd. A year ago Akeelah had suggested that maybe she could help him, and for weeks afterward he wouldn't speak to her. She realized that she'd made a mistake by insulting his dignity and pride.

"So why y'all punkin' out on the spellin' bee?" he asked.

"I ain't punkin' out."

"Mama says maybe you is. What, you afraid of all them suburban kids?"

"No."

Terrence grabbed the box.

"Hey, give it back," she said, reaching for it.

Terrence began rifling through the cards. "So how you spell all these words, anyway?"

"I study 'em," she said.

A Ford Explorer rounded the corner, blasting its horn.

"Whatevah. There's my ride."

The Explorer pulled up and Derrick-T, sporting thick sunglasses and a New York Knicks cap, looked out the passenger window from the driver's seat. "What up, Terrence? Who dat?"

"Nobody," Terrence said. "My little sister."

Derrick-T pulled down his glasses and peered at her. "What up, li'l thing? Seen you on TV. You was very pro."

Akeelah said nothing.

"You winning contests?" Derrick-T continued. "Goin' to some big one pretty soon, huh?"

Akeelah still said nothing.

"Yo, answer the man, Kee," Terrence said. "He ain't talkin' to the wind."

"You know, I won somethin' once. Fifth grade, wrote a poem. Got me a blue ribbon, can you believe it?"

Terrence snorted laughter. "You wrote a poem? Oh, that's good, man."

"Shut up, dawg. Whatcha think rap is? Poetry, man. Poetry of the streets, and I was into that at an early age." He put his head close to the window. "What's that in your hands?"

"Nothin'," Terrence said. "Just stupid words."

"Stupid words? Words ain't never stupid." He gestured toward Akeelah. "You helpin' her?"

"Naw, man. I'm goin' with you."

Derrick-T stared at Terrence and slowly shook his head. "Nah, man. Not this trip. You stay with your sis. Help her with the words."

"Why?" Terrence said, looking puzzled.

"'Cause I said so. Ain't that enough reason?"

He started to drive off when Akeelah raised her hand and shouted, "Derrick-T!"

He braked the car and looked out at Akeelah.

"I wanna read your poem."

He broke into a wide grin. "You do?" He nodded and said, "Okay. After you win the contest. That a deal?"

"Sounds good to me. But what if I don't win?"

"Maybe I'll let you read it anyway."

He drove off. Terrence and Akeelah stood watching after the Explorer for a moment, embarrassed to be together. Their lives ran on very separate tracks.

"You don't gotta help me if you don't want to. I know it's a pain for you."

He stared at her with a half grin. "I didn't say it was a pain."

"It sounded like it when you were talkin' to Derrick-T."

"He don't have to know all my business." Terrence pulled out a card and after a struggle pronounced, "'En...fran...chise...ment.'"

"You mean 'enfranchisement.'"

"Whatevah. Can you spell it?"

"Sure." She quickly spelled it and Terrence stared at her, impressed. He pulled out another word and with a smile Akeelah said, "Yup, Mama, you're right. Fifty thousand coaches."

"Say what?" said Terrence, his forehead wrinkled.

"Nothin', Terrence. Give me another word."

They walked down the street together as Terrence continued to feed her words and she continued to spell them flawlessly.

*

"Fifty thousand coaches" was not far off the mark. Over the next three days it seemed that everyone she knew grabbed her flashcards and threw words at her. Ms. Cross was waiting to grill her with words. Half the kids in her class insisted on having the honor of getting their hands on the flashcards. Even Myrna warmed to her a little.

"You are a nerd, Akeelah," she said, "but you ain't so bad a nerd."

"You want to give me a couple of words to spell?" Akeelah said.

The girl's expression brightened. "Ya don't mind?"

"Not at all. Pick out a couple of hard ones."

Myrna burst into laughter. "You think I know hard ones from easy ones? This is Myrna, girl. I ain't suddenly growed a brain."

On the way home, skipping rope as she went, the postman stopped her and asked if he could see her flashcards, which were rapidly growing in fame. He gave her two words. "I don't know how to pronounce them. I don't know what they mean. But you sure did get 'em right, Akeelah. We're all proud of you 'round here."

"Thank you, Mr. Keating."

"I've been knowin' you since you was a little-bitty thing. You was the smartest little thing I ever did see." He hesitated. "Just like your daddy."

When she reached the Korean grocery store, a block from home, she sat on a high bench, drinking a Coke and rhythmically tapping her hand on the counter while the Korean grocer read words to Akeelah. He was proud of his American accent and took any excuse to use it.

Even Steve was eager to get into the act. Relatively sober for so late in the afternoon, he sipped on a container of coffee Akeelah had bought him and screwed up his face as he tried to decipher a word.

"'Ap-teery-goattie,'" he stumbled, looking up at her.

"What?"

Steve showed her the card. "That right there. Maybe I ain't sayin' it right."

"'Apterygote,'" she said. "You really shouldn't show me the cards."

"Oh yeah, sorry," he said, taking a shaky sip of his coffee. "Head hurts."

Akeelah smiled. "Stick to the coffee, Steve," she said gently. "And I really appreciate your help."

"You're gonna do good, li'l girl. I talked to that psychic down the street—Madam Adorne? She says you're gonna go all the way."

Derrick-T's Explorer was parked at the curb down the street from her house. She tapped her hand on the hood while he and two of his homies read from the cards.

"Don't forget your poem, Derrick-T."

"Later, girl. You got a job to do first. That's our deal. You cool with that?"

"Yeah, I'm cool."

He rolled down his window and stuck out a hand. "Give me five," he said.

They slapped hands and grinned. She was beginning to think that maybe Derrick-T wasn't so bad after all. If only she could get Steve off the booze and Derrick-T off drugs.... She shook her head and smiled.

The next day the football team was practicing for the fall season in a weedy lot behind the school. One of the players called her over when she went skipping by. They sat in a circle with Akeelah continuing to jump rope as they drilled her with words.

On their porch each night, Tanya, Kiana, and Terrence (who was showing surprising enthusiasm) took turns with her flashcards. Akeelah sneaked a look at her mother and smiled, and a proud Tanya smiled back.

"How long since you missed a word?"

"About two thousand cards ago."

"That's very impressive, Akeelah."

"Not impressive enough. My goal is not to miss another word before the Nationals."

"You don't want to miss none there, either," Terrence said.

They all laughed.

"You feel confident?" Tanya said.

"More and more." Then she thought of Dr. Larabee and sighed.

As though reading her mind, Tanya said, "He's going to be in touch with you. I know he is."

*

Each evening before the sun went down, Akeelah jumped rope in her front yard, repeating words to herself as she jumped. "...P-e-l-l-u-c-i-d-i-t-y. 'Pellucidity.' I-m-p-r-e-s-a-r-i-o. 'Impresario.'" And on and on and on, until the sun had set and she was jumping rope in the dark.

Often as she jumped in the front yard, cars would drive by, horns would honk, and drivers would shout out, "You go, Akeelah! Make us proud!"

One night when she stopped jumping and was winding up the jump rope, she noticed some markings on the wooden handle. She squinted at them closely. Etched into the ends of the handles were the initials "D" and "L."

She continued to stare at the initials, her mind racing. She sat down on the front steps, still looking at the "D" and "L." Then she shook her head and said, "Well, I'll be...."

"L" for Larabee.

And the "D"?

"Denise," she muttered excitedly. "The name he called me by mistake…."

*

Akeelah slept poorly that night, tossing and turning and wrestling with her pillow. She was waiting for morning to come, and the time crawled by an agonizing moment at a time. She knew what she had to do. She had to go see Dr. Larabee. Her mother was right—her friend, her mentor, was holding something dark inside and it was festering. She wasn't sure what she could do, if anything, to help him, but she had to try. She had to accept the truth: he meant more to her than she could say—and it was way beyond spelling. He gave her confidence in herself, something she hadn't had entirely since her father's death. He made her feel that she counted. He had done so much for her since they had begun working together; the question that faced her now was, What could she do for him?

She knew that Dr. Larabee was an early riser and she arrived at his house at eight o'clock, cradling a box of flashcards in her arms. He was already at work in his garden, planting flowers. She quietly set the boxes of flashcards on the ground next to him. He glanced at them and then turned to Akeelah, a welcoming light in his eyes.

"Five thousand," Akeelah said. "Learned 'em all. But I had some help—my mom, Kiana, and Terrence, neighborhood people, and other kids, even the Crenshaw foot-

141

ball team." She grinned. "It seems like everybody wants a piece of the action."

He looked at her thoughtfully. "You should be very well prepared, then."

Akeelah nodded, then took a deep breath and plunged ahead. "You know, Dr. Larabee…a few years ago my daddy died. It hit me really hard—harder than I knew at first, but when I understood he was gone, gone forever…well, that was when things got really bad. I used to cry all the time. But then I found something that helped."

Dr. Larabee was standing with a spade in his hand, staring at her. The expression in his eyes was new to her. She wondered if it was fear.

"What was that?" he said.

"I spelled."

"You spelled?"

"Yeah. Over and over again. When I spelled words, I felt better. My daddy had always loved words, he read all the time, and I think I learned the beauty of words from him. I learned Scrabble from him when I was seven, and we used to play it all the time together."

Dr. Larabee nodded, absorbed in what she was telling him. "But I wonder why spelling words would make you feel better."

"I don't know," she said. "It just did. It seemed like words were my friends." She paused, stared directly into his eyes, and said slowly, "Maybe when you're thinking about her, you can try spelling. It might help."

He returned her stare, and now she could see the vulnerability, the hint of fear.

She reached into her pocket and pulled out the wound-up jump rope. She set it down next to the boxes. "Thanks for the loan of it, Dr. Larabee." She then turned to leave.

Dr. Larabee reached for the jump rope, saw the initials, and felt the sadness welling up in him. He called out to Akeelah's retreating back: "Wait a minute. Come back."

She stopped and turned to him.

"Who...told you?" he said.

Akeelah walked slowly back to him. "You did," she said. "You called me by her name—Denise. That's her jump rope, isn't it?"

Dr. Larabee studied the dug-up soil at his feet, his face etched with sadness. He nodded.

"Was she your little girl?"

Again he nodded.

"What happened to her, Dr. Larabee?"

It was the question he did not want to answer. He had never discussed Denise's death with anyone, and for years he had managed to keep his anguish to himself. But Akeelah's simple honesty was hard to deflect. He moved away from the garden and sat on a bench. For a moment he sat in silence while Akeelah waited for him to speak, knowing that he would, but in his own time.

"She got very, very sick," he said finally. "There was nothing the doctors could do. She was a few years younger than you when she passed."

Akeelah sat on the bench next to him. "Where's her mama?" she said.

"She lives in another city now. After it happened, my wife, Patricia, and I slowly…found things to be difficult. Denise was a shadow that blotted out any lightness and joy between us. We would look at each other and Denise was always there and somehow we blamed ourselves. Eventually we began to blame each other. All that was left for us was guilt and sorrow." He paused and cleared his throat. His voice had grown thin. "That's Patricia's garden. I've maintained it just as she would have. I guess it's a way to keep something of her in my life." He paused again. "You see, I need a lot of order in my life now. That's why I don't teach in the classroom anymore. It's too unpredictable. And this whole spelling bee thing and working so closely with you had become…unpredictable as well." He turned to her. "I don't expect you to understand that."

"But I think I do," she said. "You can't allow yourself to get too close to anybody. And maybe…you were getting too close to me."

He nodded. "You spend years building up your defenses. You simplify your life. It's a way of being able to go on."

They sat together on the bench in silence. Akeelah said finally, "Dr. Larabee? I have to tell you this, and not to put pressure on you…but it's the truth. I can't go to D.C. without you."

"Yes, you can," he said. "You can do anything you want, Akeelah. You still don't have a proper respect for your gifts."

"No. I can't beat Dylan."

144

"Don't say that. It's a way of setting yourself up for failure."

"I need you there. Don't you understand that?"

He said slowly, "I understand what you're saying."

"It's really true, Dr. Larabee. It doesn't matter how many words I learn. He'll always know more. I don't have what it takes to beat him. Especially not without you."

Dr. Larabee regarded her for a long moment.

"You know, one of the things I thought about after Denise passed…I thought that maybe the person who could have cured that horrible disease didn't do so because…he was too busy being hungry in Somalia…or oppressed in Afghanistan…or maybe he was poor in Appalachia…or dying of AIDS in Chad.…" He paused, his jaw working with emotion. "Maybe he just didn't think he 'had what it takes.'" Dr. Larabee looked into Akeelah's eyes. "Your destiny, Akeelah, lies far beyond winning any spelling bee. I hope you know that."

"Okay," she said. "But I still can't beat Dylan. Not without you."

Dr. Larabee's solemn features suddenly brightened in a smile. "Well, let me tell you about Dylan. And I want you to listen to this closely. There's only one person who can push him to spell as well as he possibly can. Only one—and that's not his dad, not the spelling bee people, and not even himself with his swollen ego and fear of his father. That person is *you*." He held her gaze as he added, "So when you and I get to Washington—let's just make sure we give him a run for his money.…"

"You and I, Dr. Larabee? Did I hear you right?"

He nodded. "You and I, Akeelah."

She clapped her hands, grinned, and gave him a big hug. She saw tears glistening in his eyes and hugged him even harder.

Twelve

Akeelah ran down the street, hopping and skipping as she went, being the eleven-year-old she sometimes forgot how to be, and bounded up the front steps of a small house. She rang the bell. When Georgia answered and saw that it was Akeelah, her eyes grew cold.

"Hey," Akeelah said. "What up?"

"Hi."

"I been callin' you a lot."

"Guess I haven't been around all that much."

"I've left a bunch of messages."

Georgia nodded but said nothing. She stood in the half-open door, not inviting Akeelah in.

"Well, I'm off to D.C. tomorrow," Akeelah said, ending an uncomfortable silence.

"Yeah, well…have fun."

"You know, Georgia, I have to say this. Everybody's been workin' with my flashcards. Did you know that?"

"Yeah," Georgia said grudgingly.

"Everybody but you. You haven't offered to help me once."

"You don't need my help."

Akeelah slowly shook her head. "Yes, I do."

"I've been too busy for that stuff," Georgia said, her voice tight.

"Look," Akeelah said, "I've been busy, too. Too busy to spend time with my best friend, which is wrong. Just…this whole spelling bee's been real intense."

Georgia nodded, her eyes still cold. "You don't need to apologize to me."

"But you know what? I'd give it all up if it meant you and me could hang out again. Friends are more important."

Georgia gave a short laugh. "That's stupid. You're doin' something nobody else can do."

"You think what I said is stupid?"

"Yeah, it is. 'Cause people wanna see you do good." She paused, and for the first time there was a flicker of life in her expression. "*I* wanna see you do good."

Akeelah smiled and reached for her friend's arm.

"You know, Georgia, you're the best friend I've ever had, and you always tell me I can do things even when I think I can't. Well, I gotta tell you something. If you wanna be a flight attendant, you first gotta ride in an airplane."

"I will someday."

"Yeah? Well, how 'bout tomorrow? Is that too soon?"

She smiled and held up a plane ticket. She handed it to Georgia, who stared at it for a moment, frowning, and then broke into a mile-wide smile.

*

Akeelah had never seen her mother move so fast. She cleaned the house and paid for a taxi so that her brother Ralph could come stay with Terrence and keep an eye on him (Kiana and Terrence did not get along) and packed a suitcase for herself and one for Akeelah. She had worked two extra weekend shifts to satisfy her bosses, who were not happy about giving her time off, as the hospital was severely short-staffed. She made an enormous lunch to take on the plane over Akeelah's protests, and at the last minute she called five of her closest friends and told them, without bragging but with a hint of pride, that the principal of Crenshaw Middle School, Mr. Welch, had actually purchased her round-trip ticket himself. Wasn't that the sweetest thing for the man to do?

She and Akeelah were up at the crack of dawn and into a taxi to the airport more than an hour ahead of schedule. When Akeelah walked up the ramp to the interior of the plane, she felt a sense of wonder. She was not only flying for the first time in her life, but was leaving the state of California for the first time in her life and going all the way across America. She was on her way to Washington, D.C.! She was on her way to the National Spelling Bee! Her mother was right. She understood it now. Win or lose, her participation in the bee was a win all the way.

When the airplane raced down the runway and took off gracefully like an enormous bird, she pressed her face to the window and watched the checkerboard world spread out below. She drew in a breath and muttered to herself, "Girl, is this really happening to you? On a plane across the country?" She had dreamed about making it to D.C. for so long that the fact of it actually happening, *here and now, in this present moment,* no longer seemed entirely real to her.

Georgia came rushing along the aisle and plumped herself down next to Akeelah.

"They let me sit in the cockpit for, like, two minutes," she gushed. "Forget flight attendant. I'm gonna be a pilot."

"That's right, girl. Aim high."

Georgia pumped her fist and laughed. "That's right. I'm gonna aim as high as this plane can fly."

"And hope the passengers do not die."

"Not with me at the controls flying the friendly sky."

Georgia nodded. "Thass right. And you don't lie."

They broke up laughing.

Hours later, when the plane was beginning its descent into Dulles Airport, the girls heard a moaning sound from across the aisle. They quit chatting and stared at Javier, who was leaning his head against the seat in front of him. "I know we're diving directly toward D.C.," he said to the seat. "I know it. It's time to become a man of prayer. It's my only chance. Cover all your bases, Javier. You're gonna need 'em."

"What's wrong with him?" Georgia said.

"He has an aversion to flying. Takeoffs, landings, and also while in the air," Akeelah answered.

Javier shook his head. "It's an aversion to plummeting. A fiery descent to earth when the pilot loses control. I may puke."

"My brother's in the Air Force," Akeelah said. "He says fear is all in the head."

150

"You coulda fooled me. I'd say it's in the head, the stomach, and every nerve of your body."

"Here. Devon gave me this for luck." Akeelah removed an Air Force wings pin from her shirt. She reached over to pin it to his tennis shirt. "I'll try not to impale you." He kept his eyes closed and breathed in short gasps. "You know, Javier, I never really thanked you for helpin' me out at the State Bee."

"No biggie."

"Actually, it was very chivalrous of you."

He answered with a loud groan.

"Don't be so dramatic."

"I can't help it. I'm dying."

"No, you're not. Maybe this will help." She leaned across the aisle and kissed him on the cheek.

His eyes popped open and he turned to her. "Wow. This must be what's meant by a miracle. I'm not thinking about the plane at all now, about missing the airstrip. I think I just reached heaven."

"Really?" Akeelah said with a smile. "Well, in that case..."

She flung open the window shade next to Javier, and he let out a howl of anguish as the plane lowered its landing gear.

The baggage area was a circus of yelling and laughter as the spellers collected their luggage. A chauffeur carrying a sign reading "National Spelling Bee Finalists" opened the door of a stretch limousine. Georgia stared at the rich interior and said to Akeelah in a whisper, "If I flunk out as a pilot, I can always get a license to drive one of these babies."

"I think that's called lowered expectations," Akeelah said. "Keep your eye on the sky."

As the limousine drove past the Capitol building, the Washington Monument, the Lincoln Memorial, and the White House, Akeelah was dumbstruck. She was vaguely aware that Georgia was burbling on about something, but her mind was elsewhere. History was all around her. She pressed her face to the window and absorbed it all. She knew that she was living in a dream, and it was a dream from which she didn't want to awaken.

They registered at the hotel, and later that day, she was beside herself with excitement when she learned that she and a group of other spellers were scheduled to take a tour of the West Wing of the White House.

"Will I meet the President?" Akeelah asked the tour director.

"I'm afraid he's out of town," he said with a smile. "But the First Lady will greet you all."

There was actually a receiving line to walk through. Suddenly Akeelah was pressing the warm, soft hand of the First Lady and returning her bright smile.

"I've read about you," the First Lady said. "You're Akeelah Anderson from California."

"Yes, ma'am."

"I wish you the best of luck in the National Bee."

"Well, that makes two of us. I'm wishing myself the best of luck, too."

The First Lady laughed and Akeelah blushed, wondering if she had just said something incredibly stupid.

The hours flew by. Inside the Frederick Douglass National Historic Site, Akeelah and a group of other young spellers read one of the speeches by the famous abolitionist. Suddenly Dr. Larabee stepped up behind her, smiled, and they read it together.

"How do you feel?" he said.

"I don't know. What's that thing—you know, out-of-body experience? That's what I think I'm having. I'm just floating."

"That must be a good feeling."

"Yeah, I guess. It's kind of scary."

He scrutinized her carefully. "You look well rested. And I like your outfit."

She beamed. "You do? Mama picked out three for me and the school paid for them. Next stop will be the cover of *Vogue*."

"Or *Harper's Bazaar*."

The day was sunny, with none of Washington's usual summer humidity, and Akeelah and Dr. Larabee began walking back to the hotel. It was a long walk, but they were in the mood for exercise. After they had walked a while, Akeelah's hand stole into Dr. Larabee's. He gave no indication that he was aware of it, but he did not pull his hand away.

"So do you think you're ready for the big event?"

She hesitated before shaking her head up and down. "As ready as I'll ever be. I know I'm up against a bunch of genius spellers. But I don't let that bother me. I'm pretty good myself."

"You're better than pretty good, Akeelah. You have the mental architecture for this—visualization, memory, patterns, a great eye and ear." He glanced at her. "I wonder what kind of chess player you'd make. I'd be willing to give you some lessons."

"I'd love that!" she said, delighted to hear from his own lips that their relationship would not end once the National Bee was over. "I always wanted to learn."

"Well, then, that's next on the agenda."

They returned to the hotel just as a press conference was beginning. Akeelah sat with a dozen other spellers in a small room off the lobby where reporters bombarded them with questions and photographers snapped pictures. When Dylan was asked about his chances to win the National, he gave the camera a serious look and said, "Well, I've been second twice in a row. Don't they say that practice makes perfect?" His eye still on the camera, he broke into a boyish grin.

"Yuck," Javier said. "Double yuck."

"Shh," Akeelah said, nudging him in the side.

When Javier was asked the same question, he said, "I play to win but I'm prepared to lose."

"A reasonable position," Dylan whispered loudly enough for Javier to hear. The two boys locked glances.

That night, in Akeelah and Georgia's room, Javier popped open an Orange Crush and the soda fizzed across the carpet. The girls ducked for cover, Georgia laughing hysterically. They were all in their pajamas.

"Dummy," Akeelah said. "I told you not to shake it. Didn't anybody ever teach you that?"

Javier burst into hysterical laughter as he wiped soda from his face with his pajama sleeve. "I'm not teachable, don't you know that? I just do what comes naturally, and it isn't always so natural."

"I've noticed."

Hearing the noise from the adjoining room, Tanya opened the door to the girls' room and strode in.

"Akeelah, I thought you were studying. What's going on?"

"We are!" She giggled. "But we're also trying to relax."

"Sounds like a war party to me. You got a big day tomorrow, so say goodnight."

"Half an hour more. *Please,* Mama."

"Yes, Mama," Javier said, grinning. "*Please.*"

Tanya could not restrain a chuckle. "Well, okay. Fifteen minutes." Shaking her head, she disappeared into the next room.

"What do you think Dylan's doing now?" Akeelah asked, turning to Javier.

"Trying to learn ancient Greek. Praying in tongues. Giving Mr. Watanabe a back rub."

"Maybe we should invite him over."

"That jerk? Forget it. Besides, we've got curfew in fifteen minutes."

Akeelah grabbed a soda and headed for the door.

"Hey, where you goin'?" said Javier, struggling out of the deep couch to his feet.

"You'll see."

Akeelah padded down the hall in her pajamas. She came to Room 217, hesitated, took a deep breath, and knocked. After a moment, Mr. Watanabe opened the door, stared at Akeelah briefly, and then looked away.

"Uh…hi…. Is Dylan, ah, available?"

She saw him sitting at a table overflowing with word lists and dictionaries. He looked up and then quickly buried his nose in a book.

"He's busy," Mr. Watanabe said.

"Well, me and some of the other kids are hanging out in my room drinking soda pop and watching movies. We thought maybe he'd wanna come over. You know, break the tension a little."

Unable to stifle his irritation, Mr. Watanabe said sharply, "That's not possible. Tomorrow's the spelling bee."

"Yeah, that's what I mean. Sometimes it's good to take a little rest, veg out a little right before the big event, ya know?"

Mr. Watanabe shook his head and frowned. "Perhaps that's your strategy. It certainly is not ours."

He started to close the door when Akeelah held out the Orange Crush. "Hey, this is for Dylan. Keep him company while he works."

Mr. Watanabe hesitated before snatching the soda from her. Akeelah caught a glimpse of Dylan staring at her just before the door slammed shut. She couldn't be sure she wasn't reading too much into it, but she thought she saw puzzlement and sadness clouding his face.

Thirteen

Akeelah woke up feeling wired, ready to leap out of her skin. Yet deep inside, her mind was calm. She felt ready. She made her way through the crowd of people and cameras like a prizefighter making her way to the ring. She nodded to Dylan but he looked away. As Akeelah ascended the stage with Javier, Dylan, and 200 other spellers and took her seat, she remembered the words Dr. Larabee had forced her to memorize at the beginning of the summer: *We ask ourselves, Who am I to be brilliant, gorgeous, talented, and fabulous? Actually, who are you* not *to be those things?*

In the audience, Dr. Larabee sat with Tanya, Georgia, Mr. Welch, and Devon, who was beaming with pride and decked out in his Air Force regalia. A row in front of them, Mr. Watanabe sat rigid and nervous, kneading his hands in his lap.

Her eyes sought out Dr. Larabee's and he answered her gaze with a small smile.

At first I was doing this for Daddy. Now I'm doing it for you. Yes, I want to win, I want to win more than anything, but I'm doing this for you, Dr. Larabee. I wonder if you know that.

A well-dressed television announcer, Ted Saunders, spoke into the TV monitor in a soundproof booth above

157

the auditorium. "Hello," he said in a deep, melodious announcer's voice, "and welcome to the Scripps National Spelling Bee." He flashed a bright, practiced grin. "I'm Ted Saunders here with Margaret Russell, broadcasting live from the main ballroom of the Grand Hyatt Washington, where today's winner will take home the champion's trophy and prize money worth…twenty thousand dollars!" He turned to his colleague, and his smile beamed up to an even brighter wattage. "Now, Margaret, as a former spelling bee finalist yourself, what should we be looking for in this year's bee? Any predictions?"

"Well, there are several kids who placed very high in last year's competition, most notably Dylan Watanabe. In fact, he has finished second in the last two National Bees. I would say he's the odds-on favorite to win this year. But spelling bees are notoriously unpredictable. The children are young, and new geniuses break through on a regular basis." She paused as the camera panned over the young contestants. "But the speller I've really got my eye on is little Akeelah Anderson from Los Angeles. This is her first year in competition and she shows great promise."

Akeelah's image appeared on a huge-projection TV.

"She looks more like nine than eleven," Saunders observed. "But I see determination written all over her."

Margaret Russell continued: "Akeelah has become a bit of a media sensation. This is, as I said, the eleven-year-old's first try at the spelling bee circuit."

When Akeelah's name was called, Javier said, "Break a leg. Break two for luck!"

When she got up from her chair and smiled at Javier, she could tell that he was as nervous as she was. Standing at the mike, she looked out at the sea of lights and cameras. She closed her eyes, fighting for calm, and when she opened them hundreds of people were staring back at her. *Calm yourself, girl. You know how good you are. You are here to make Daddy proud. And Dr. Larabee. And Mama. And Devon and Kiana and Terrence and Georgia and everybody who helped you learn to spell all those words. And maybe most of all, girl, you are here to make* you *proud.*

She caught Dr. Larabee's eye in the audience and his eyes were steady and reassuring as he nodded to her. She nodded back. She glanced at the Pronouncer, a professorial-looking man who, with an assistant beside him, sat at a table near the long panel of Judges, including the Head Judge.

"'Ratiocinate,'" the Pronouncer said.

"Could you repeat the word, please?" Akeelah said.

"'Ratiocinate.'"

"I'd like a definition."

"To reason logically and methodically," the Pronouncer said.

Akeelah began to beat lightly on her left thigh.

"'Ratiocinate,'" she said slowly. "R-a-t-i-o-c-i-n-a-t-e. 'Ratiocinate.'"

She rushed back to her seat.

As the bee completed its first thirty minutes, Ted

Saunders, still wearing a bright smile, said, "Wow, these kids are something else."

Margaret Russell turned to him. "But watch out, Ted. Single elimination is ruthless. One wrong letter and that's it."

Another speller was eliminated when she misspelled "paramatta." Akeelah whispered to Javier, "She's too good a speller to miss that. The double consonant was so obvious, don't you think?"

"Yeah, an easy word," Javier agreed.

Turning to Margaret Russell, Saunders said, "You might want to explain how they determine the winner."

"It's whoever's left standing," she replied. "But the final speller *must* spell the last word missed—plus an *additional* word—or the competition continues."

Dylan took the mike and gave Akeelah a barely perceptible glance. She stared at him and then looked away. He spelled his word with no trouble and slowly ambled back to his seat.

Ted Saunders said, "These kids are fabulous. I thought I was a decent speller, but now I know better. This could go on forever."

"Well, once there are only two players left, they begin with the twenty-five championship-level words, which are so difficult someone always misses one."

"You mean *these words* are not championship-caliber?"

"Oh, yes. But the twenty-five are at the highest end of difficulty."

On Dylan's next turn at the mike, the Pronouncer said, "The word is 'oersted.'"

Dylan stared at him, expressionless. Mr. Watanabe suddenly shifted forward in his chair. "What's the language of origin?" Dylan said.

"Danish," said the Pronouncer.

Dylan nodded. "I'd like a definition, please."

The Pronouncer looked carefully at a card in his hand. "The centimeter-gram-second electromagnetic unit of magnetic intensity equal to the magnetic intensity one centimeter from a unit magnetic pole."

There was a rumble in the audience.

Ted Saunders turned to Margaret Russell. "Did you understand that definition?"

"I plead the Fifth," she said, smiling.

"O-e-r-s-t-e-d," Dylan said quickly. "'Oersted.'"

The audience broke into applause. Akeelah saw Dylan glance down at his father, who betrayed no emotion. Dylan looked away and slowly took his seat.

Javier was now at the mike.

"The word is 'xylem.'"

"X-y-l-e-m. 'Xylem.'"

Mr. and Mrs. Mendez applauded their son. Akeelah gave him a big smile when he returned to his seat. They slapped hands between their seats.

"They thought they had me—but I was too much for 'em."

Akeelah laughed.

"You wanna know a secret?"

"Yeah."

161

"I learned that word last week." He wiped his forehead in a mock-relief gesture. "Just in the nick of time."

The opening rounds of the spelling bee were a showcase for the expert spellers and a bloodbath for the others. Spellers battled one difficult word after another. The kids had all kinds of ways of coping: some of them wrote the words in the air, some turned in circles, rolled their eyes, held their breath. Akeelah was alone in tapping her thigh. They all asked for definitions, alternate pronunciations, and languages of origin. Akeelah, Dylan, Javier, and a handful of others successfully navigated through the first rounds to the delight of their families and fans.

A boy in a wheelchair was now at the mike, one of a scattering of survivors.

Margaret Russell looked intensely into the TV monitor. "Here in the eighth round of the National Spelling Bee, with only sixteen spellers remaining, Peter Adams is faced with the word 'excursus.'" She turned to Ted Saunders. "Not an easy word."

"No, indeed not."

"E-x-c-o-u-r-s-e-s. 'Excursus.'..." He looked fearfully at the Head Judge and then heard the bell sound. He shrugged as he motored away from the mike. "Hey," he said, loud enough for the audience to hear. "Sixteenth place. Not bad!"

He popped a wheelie in his chair and rode off the stage, getting a big laugh from the crowd.

Javier leaned over and whispered to Akeelah, "Peter is cool. I really like him."

"He reminds me of you," Akeelah said.

162

It was her turn to step up to the mike. Each round took her closer to her goal, and each time felt more difficult than the time before.

Ted Saunders said, "Here is Akeelah Anderson up to attempt her eighth word."

"The word is 'argillaceous,'" the Pronouncer said.

Akeelah stared at him, then sneaked a quick look at Dr. Larabee. It was clear to him that she had never heard of the word. "Excuse me?" Her hand remained frozen at her side.

"'Argillaceous,'" the Pronouncer repeated.

"Can I get a definition, please?" she said.

"Like or containing clay," he said.

Tanya strained forward in her seat, holding tightly to the hands of both Devon and Georgia. It was obvious that Akeelah was struggling for the first time.

"What's the language of origin?" Akeelah asked, still not moving her hand.

A bad sign, Dr. Larabee thought, as he tried to keep his composure.

"Greek," the Pronouncer answered.

"It's the suffix that could trip her up," Margaret Russell said. "Most people would spell it 'tious' or 'cious.' A very, very tricky word, indeed."

"You can see the strain on her face," Ted Saunders observed.

Dr. Larabee muttered loudly enough for Mr. Welch to hear, "Come on, Akeelah. See it. *See* it."

Akeelah stared at him again and something was communicated between them. She turned to the Pronouncer.

"Is it derived from the Greek word 'argos,' meaning white?"

Dr. Larabee nodded. She was on the right track. If only she could keep her nerve and think logically and straight. This word was not too big for her. Others might be, but not "argillaceous."

Akeelah scrunched up her face and thought hard. She remembered Dr. Larabee standing next to his huge pad full of words and pointing to one, and she strained to remember that word. In her mind's eye she saw "argilla," but she couldn't see the ending. She sensed that the danger lay in the ending.

The Head Judge motioned to her. "You've exhausted your regular time, Ms. Anderson. You now have thirty seconds of finish time to spell the word."

She nodded as her hand began to flutter and finally touched her thigh. She began moving back and forth rhythmically. Javier bit his lip, his eyes fixed on her. Dylan leaned back in his chair and closed his eyes, the faintest of smiles on his lips.

"'Argillaceous,'" Akeelah said finally. Her fingers began counting on her thigh. "A…r…g…i…l… l…a…." Her fingers slowed, paused. She could see all the faces staring at her, the world closing in on her, the bright lights blazing in her eyes. She felt a wave of faintness.

"Can I start over?"

"You may," said the Head Judge. "But you cannot change the letters you've already spelled."

Dr. Larabee and Mr. Welch exchanged worried glances. Georgia covered her eyes, overwhelmed by the

164

tension. Tanya sat straight and still, as though she were meditating.

Akeelah put her feet together, forced herself to breathe deeply, and made her hand stop fluttering. She kept her eyes ahead, took a moment, and then started jumping up and down. There were looks and murmurs of confusion in the audience. What was this girl doing?

Dr. Larabee nodded and turned to Mr. Welch. "She sees the word now. She's pretending to jump rope."

"But why?"

"Because that's how she visualizes."

"A-r-g-i-l-l-a...," she said slowly, in time with the jumps. She remembered now—Dr. Larabee standing at his desk slapping the pad of paper with his pointer. The pointer fell on...*yes!*

"...c-e-o-u-s. 'Argillaceous.'"

She stopped jumping. There was no bell.

The applause in the audience was deafening, and Mr. Welch actually jumped out of his chair and pumped his fist. Dr. Larabee gave a quiet nod of satisfaction. "Good girl," he said softly. "You knew what to do. You didn't panic."

Akeelah sat down and let out an exhausted breath. She saw Dylan stare at her intently and then slowly look away.

Ted Saunders, looking more serious now, said, "It's the twelfth round now, folks. And the five remaining spellers are Mary Calveretti, age thirteen, of Tulsa, Oklahoma...fourteen-year-old Rajeev Subramonian of New York City...thirteen-year-old Javier Mendez of

Woodland Hills, California…Dylan Watanabe, also from Woodland Hills. Wow, they really crank 'em out on the Left Coast, don't they? And, of course, Akeelah Anderson of Los Angeles."

Javier strolled to the mike, grinning to cover his nervousness.

"The word is 'Merovingian,'" said the Pronouncer.

Javier scratched his head, drawing a titter from the audience. "Could you use the word in a sentence, please?"

"The Merovingian kings were known for having long red hair."

Akeelah bit her lip, feeling Javier's tension.

"Okay…uh…M-a-r-a-v-i-n-g-i-a-n? 'Merovingian.'"

The bell sounded and Akeelah gasped. Mrs. Mendez put her hands to her mouth.

"The correct spelling," said the Pronouncer, "is M-*e*-r-*o*-v-i-n-g-i-a-n."

Javier gave the audience a showman's bow, deep and with a sweep of the hand. The audience laughed and applauded one of their favorite contestants. As Javier left the stage, he turned to Akeelah.

"I forgot to spell how it sounds. The very thing I told you never to do, and then I go and do it. But hey—thirteenth last year, no worse than fifth this year—next time I take it all! Now it's *your* turn. I'm depending on you."

Akeelah smiled and her eyes followed Javier as he shuffled off the stage.

Now Mary Calveretti, a brunette with a thick

Southern accent, minced up to the mike and offered a subtle curtsy as she smiled out at the audience.

"'Mithridatism,'" said the Pronouncer.

You could see her face fall as her mind grappled with the word's various possibilities.

"Could you give me the meanin'?"

"Tolerance for a poison by taking ever larger doses."

"M-i-t-h-r-o-d-a-t-i-s-m. 'Mithridatism.'"

The bell went *ding!* and the girl slouched offstage, her eyes glued to the floor.

Dylan was up next and made short work of "resipiscence." He shot a quick glance at Akeelah as he returned to his seat. She saw something in his eyes she hadn't seen before—something speculative and thoughtful. She wondered if it was respect.

Rajeev Subramonian approached the mike, rubbing his hands nervously. With a slight Indian accent, he slowly spelled "vitrophyre," spelling the last four letters as "f-i-e-r."

Dylan glanced at Akeelah, one eyebrow raised, as if to say, "Rajeev blew an easy one."

The Indian boy obviously didn't agree. "That sucks out loud," he grumbled as he left the stage.

Finally it was Akeelah's turn, and the importance of this round did not escape her. If she spelled the word correctly, it would be between her and Dylan.

"The word is 'serpiginous,'" the Pronouncer said.

"I would like a definition, please."

"A spreading skin eruption or disease," said the Pronouncer.

Akeelah nodded and said calmly, "S-e-r-p-i-g-i-n-o-u-s. 'Serpiginous.'"

The bell did not ring, and Akeelah returned to her seat. Devon stood up and gave a shrill whistle through his teeth, and the audience clapped much more boisterously than for Dylan. She was clearly the audience favorite. She sat down and closed her eyes. *I'm here,* she thought. *I'm knockin' on the door. Don't lose your cool, girl. Just don't you dare lose your cool.*

The Head Judge stood at the mike and said, "As we're down to our final two spellers, we're going to take a small break before Ms. Anderson and Mr. Watanabe commence with the championship-level words. We will resume in fifteen minutes."

Akeelah raced to the bathroom and dashed cold water on her face. She looked at herself in the mirror and smiled proudly at her image. "Daddy, how'm I doin'?" She pursed her lips in a kiss and then turned and left.

Outside the door she heard voices raised and she recognized the loud angry ranting of Mr. Watanabe coming from the men's room.

"This is your last spelling bee, Dylan. Just remember one thing. You let that girl win and you're second place your whole life. But there's no way we are going to allow that to happen, is there? You hear me? *Look* at me when I'm speaking to you. We didn't work this hard for this long for second place. *No way,* do you understand me?"

The harshness in his tone made Akeelah flinch.

"You listening in on conversations?"

Akeelah turned with a start and saw Dr. Larabee standing there.

Trying to grin she said, "I'm wishing Dylan good luck. I mean mentally. His dad gives him a real rough time."

"He's a typical stage parent. They invest their lives in their children and it becomes a disease." He paused and then reached for her hand. "You've done a superb job. I'm very proud of you, Akeelah."

"Thank you." She felt a blush on her cheeks but fought to keep her cool. They started walking back to the ballroom together.

"This is the ninth inning now," Dr. Larabee said. "Or maybe extra innings is more apt. You think it's been hard so far—just wait. They're going to hit you with every trick word they've got now. No mercy. But you've studied them all, or words akin to the words they'll give you. You'll do fine."

Akeelah turned back and saw Mr. Watanabe lead a sullen Dylan out of the men's room.

"But, Dr. Larabee, if I don't beat Dylan—I still have next year, right?"

"Of course you do. But I don't know how much time we'll have to train together. I just accepted an offer to go back and teach at UCLA."

"Really? That's fabulous!" She squeezed his hand and smiled up at him. "Maybe I'll sit in on one of your classes. Could I?"

"Of course you could. But knowing you, you'd want to take over and start teaching the course."

Her grin grew wider. "Maybe…."

As Mr. Watanabe and Dylan marched by them, without a glance in their direction, Watanabe sternly lectured his son. Akeelah looked down and sighed.

"Akeelah, what is it?" Dr. Larabee said, sensing her stiffen.

She hesitated before saying, "Nothing, Dr. Larabee. I should get back. No matter what happens—win or lose—I just want you to know I couldn't have gotten this far without you."

Before he could respond, she scampered off to the staging area. Dr. Larabee looked perplexed; he sensed that something was wrong but he had no idea what.

Ted Saunders was saying to the TV audience, "Now keep in mind, if either speller misses a word, the other has to spell the missed one plus another to win."

Margaret Russell nodded. "And, of course, they could exhaust all twenty-five championship words."

"Has that ever happened?"

"No, not all twenty-five."

"But for argument's sake, let's say they managed to spell all the championship words correctly. What would be the next step, Margaret?"

"Well, they would be co-champions," she replied, "but that's never happened before, as I said. The championship words are just too difficult."

As Akeelah and Dylan took the stage, the crowd burst into applause. The seats were packed with spectators; the atmosphere was electric with anticipation. Everyone was expecting an exciting battle to the end. Akeelah smiled at the ovation, bowing her head slightly. But Dylan stood there stiffly, unsmiling, watching his father staring at him with his arms folded. Akeelah saw Watanabe's icy demeanor and glanced worriedly at Dylan. Akeelah's feelings toward Dylan had changed since they arrived in Washington. She was no longer bothered by his arrogance, which she considered a front, a protection against his father's cold perfectionism. More and more she had come to realize how hard it must be to live Dylan's life, how little joy he was allowed to feel, and her heart had begun to go out to him. Did she like him? Yes. In a strange way she had come to appreciate his intelligence and to take on his problems as her own—a sure sign of friendship.

The Head Judge said, "Ms. Anderson, you're up first."

She looked from Dylan to Dr. Larabee, whose eyes were on her intently, and then to the Head Judge. She moved slowly to the mike.

"The word is 'xanthosis,'" said the Pronouncer.

Akeelah looked at him, startled, and then glanced back at Dylan, who was peering at her sharply. Her mind suddenly flashed back to the chemistry room in Woodland Hills. *"Spell 'xanthosis,'"* Dylan had demanded, *and Akeelah had said, "z-a-n—" and Dylan had said, "It starts with an 'x.'"*

It was as clear to her as though it had happened yesterday. Akeelah never forgot a misspelled word—and especially that word under those circumstances.

She continued to stare at Dylan and she could tell from his expression that he knew she knew the word.

"Would you like me to repeat the word?" said the Pronouncer.

She cleared her throat nervously. "'Xanthosis'?"

"That's correct."

Akeelah saw Mr. Watanabe, arms crossed over his jacket, burning holes into his son with his dark eyes. She struggled with what to do. Her body was uncharacteristically still.

"Ms. Anderson," the Head Judge said. "Akeelah?"

"'Xanthosis,'" she said. And then slowly started to spell: "Z-a-n..."

Dylan looked up with a start, his mouth open. This wasn't possible. Something was wrong.

In the audience, Dr. Larabee rose from his chair, shocked.

"...-t-h-o-s-i-s. 'Xanthosis.'" Her eyes were glued to the mike.

If I don't beat Dylan, I still have next year...right?

The bell sounded. A groan of disappointment rose from the audience, with the exception of Mr. Watanabe, who pumped his fist in elation.

"I'm sorry, Akeelah," the Head Judge said, and he did look sincerely sorry. "That is incorrect."

She nodded and then glanced at Dr. Larabee. Seeing his shock, she quickly looked away and then went to stand next to Dylan.

The Head Judge waited for Dylan to approach the mike and when he didn't, he said, "Dylan? It's your turn."

The stupefied Dylan was still staring at Akeelah, but she wouldn't look at him. He wanted to read her expression, to understand what was happening. He was skilled at processing events and analyzing them, but now he was completely confused. Finally she turned to him and gave a little gesture to take the mike. He could read nothing in her eyes. He hesitated and then stepped to the microphone.

Ted Saunders said gravely to the TV audience, "Dylan Watanabe could take it right here."

The Pronouncer said, "'Xanthosis.'"

Dylan glanced back at Akeelah, but her eyes were glued intently to the floor. He tried to slow his racing mind. He now understood what Akeelah had done. He turned back to the mike.

"'Xanthosis.'" He paused for a long moment and then began to spell: "X-a-n-t-h-o-s…e-s…. 'Xanthosis.'"

There was a *ding!* and the room was deafeningly silent after an initial intake of breath. Mr. Watanabe sprang up from his chair, outraged. Akeelah shook her head when Dylan turned to her.

"'Xanthosis' is spelled x-a-n-t-h-o-s-*i*-s," the Pronouncer said.

"Um…could I get some water, please?" Dylan showed no emotion, no disappointment. He simply stood there as though nothing at all had happened, as though he was not aware that his dream once again might have been thwarted.

The Head Judge waved a hand. "Can we bring both spellers some water?"

Dylan took advantage of this brief pause to walk back to Akeelah. He whispered furiously in her ear.

"What are you doing?"

"What are *you* doing?"

"You threw that word. You *threw* it."

"So did you."

"Come on, Akeelah. 'Xanthosis' with a 'z'? I gave you that word and you misspelled it, and I know you. There's no way in the world you'd misspell it twice." He locked his eyes onto hers. "You're just gonna give this away? Is that what you plan to do?"

"Your dad will be happy."

Dylan drew in a deep breath and whispered, "Who cares? Who *cares*? He never won anything in his life. I've got three Regional first-place titles and two seconds in the Nationals. I'm doing okay."

"And now you can have a *first,*" Akeelah said. "I can do it next year."

"No way. I don't need any help from you."

"I didn't say you did."

"You've got to do your best *this* year. There may never be another chance."

"Dylan…" She implored him with her eyes. "We're even now, okay? Whatever happens from now on, that's up to us. But I couldn't spell that word."

"I couldn't spell it, either."

Her lip curled in the hint of a smile.

"Well, you see?"

He gripped her elbow. "You do your best or I don't want it. I mean it, Akeelah."

"I'll do my best. I promise."

Ted Saunders leaned toward the TV monitor and

intoned, "Pretty amazing. Both spellers stumbled on the same word."

Margaret Russell nodded. "I think we have a couple of very nervous kids up there. Trust me on this, Ted. The stress is simply unbearable."

Akeelah came back to the mike and her word was "effleurage."

She looked at Dr. Larabee, who had returned to his seat, gave a slight nod, and began tapping on her thigh. "E-f-f-l-e-u-r-a-g-e. 'Effleurage.'"

The applause was deafening. As she stepped behind Dylan he nodded as if to say: "That's more like it." He took the mike.

Ted Saunders said, "Well, now it's like watching two star tennis players at the net returning volleys, everything on the line. You can cut the suspense with a knife."

"The word is 'lagniappe,'" said the Pronouncer to Dylan.

He frowned and closed his eyes for a moment. "A definition, please."

"A small gift presented to a customer who has made a purchase."

Dylan looked at the ceiling as he said quickly, "L-a-g-n-i-a-p-p-e. 'Lagniappe.'"

Akeelah stepped to the mike and the Pronouncer said, "The word is 'sumpsimus.'"

She nodded. "S-u-m-p-s-i-m-u-s. 'Sumpsimus.'"

"That was just a good guess," she whispered to Dylan as he approached the mike. "Never heard of the word."

He returned her grin.

175

The words kept coming and they continued to spell them correctly: "ophelimity" and "tralatitious" and "sophrosyne" and "parrhesia" and "lyophilize" and "zarzuela" and "vibrissae" and "craquelure." Sometimes they asked for the correct part of speech or the word's proper use in a sentence or its language of origin, but they were full of confidence and rarely hesitated. It was an amazing performance and the audience was totally caught up in the contest, applauding and cheering and whistling and stomping their feet.

"These two are chewing through these words like they're breakfast cereal," Ted Saunders exclaimed.

"It's a brilliant display," Margaret Russell agreed. "Two extremely well trained spellers who have done their homework and then some. But there's more to it than that. They are intuitive and they can *see* the words, they have actual shapes, almost like Chinese ideograms. This is not some rote trick, Ted. This is very subtle art you're seeing."

Dr. Larabee was now pacing in the back of the ballroom, wearing a nervous smile. Mr. Welch, who could no longer sit still, joined his old college friend.

"She's holding up, Josh," Mr. Welch said.

"Yes. If anything, she's growing stronger, more confident." He looked thoughtful. "There's more here than meets the eye."

"What do you mean?"

"Something between Akeelah and the Watanabe kid. It has to do with the word they both misspelled. I hate to say it, but I think they misspelled it deliberately.

176

'Xanthosis' is not all that difficult a word. They would both see right through the 'x'-'z' trick."

"But why on earth would they do that?"

Dr. Larabee shrugged. "I have no idea, and I have a feeling we're never going to know. My guess is, it's their secret—one they don't plan to share with anybody."

Speaking directly into the camera's eye, Margaret Russell said, "You know, Ted, they could actually go the distance—all twenty-five championship words. Most people consider that *unthinkable*."

"Well, it looks like they've got a great chance," Saunders said. "I don't see any stumbling or nervousness. They're in a groove."

Dylan started to leave the mike after spelling his word correctly when the Head Judge raised a hand. "Just one second, Dylan. We're thirteen words into the championship and it's now time to switch the order. You will now get another word."

Dylan nodded and said, "All right."

The Head Judge continued, saying, "Now I'm sure you both realize that if you each make it through the remaining twelve words, you will emerge as co-champions. That has never happened before."

Dylan looked back at Akeelah and something secret, known only to the two of them, passed between them.

"Your word is 'vinegarroon,'" the Pronouncer said to Dylan.

"'Vinegarroon.' V-i-n-e-g-a-r-r-o-o-n," Dylan answered with no hesitation.

"'Ecdysis,'" the Pronouncer said to Akeelah.

She started slowly tapping her thigh, but hesitated to begin. Dylan leaned forward in his chair, gazing at her intently.

"A definition, please?"

"The shedding of an outer layer of skin, as in insects or snakes."

"The language of origin?"

"Greek."

Akeelah nodded and her tapping grew more rhythmic, her head bobbing slightly. "'Ecdysis,'" she said. "E-c-d-y-s-i-s."

She returned to her chair, whispering quickly to Dylan, "Almost had brain lock."

He smiled and quickly spelled his word: "concitato."

"The word is 'puerpera,'" the Pronouncer said to Akeelah.

"'Puerpera'?"

"That's right."

"Fever," she whispered under her breath.

The Head Judge leaned forward. "Excuse me?"

"'Puerpera,'" Akeelah said. "P-u-e-r-p-e-r-a."

Dylan grinned and gave her a high five as he went to the mike.

Ted Saunders said, "Dylan and Akeelah are trying to stage a miracle here. They seem unaware of the degree of difficulty these words present."

"That's true," Margaret Russell replied. "And to make it to the finish line, they need each other to succeed."

But suddenly, for the first time, Dylan was struggling.

He ran a finger across his brow and frowned. He cleared his throat and said, "Would you repeat the word, please?"

"'Scheherazadian.'"

"'Scheherazadian,'" Dylan repeated.

Seconds passed. Akeelah leaned forward in her chair, muttering, "Come on, come *on*...."

Finally Dylan said, "S-c-h-e-h-e-r-a-z-a-d-i-a-n. 'Scheherazadian.'"

"Yes!" Akeelah said out loud.

Dylan let out a sighing breath and returned to his seat, giving Akeelah a quick eye roll as though to say, *Whew! I just dodged the bullet.*

"Go get 'em," he whispered.

Akeelah took the mike.

"'Palynological.'"

She started tapping her thigh and then hesitated. She stared at Dr. Larabee, who sat perfectly still, not moving a muscle.

"Definition, please?"

Dylan shifted in his seat nervously and lifted his crossed fingers to his lips.

"Concerned with pollen or pollen grains."

Akeelah swiveled her hips slightly, rolled her eyes, and said, "Oh, that sure helps."

There was a whisper of strained laughter from the audience.

"Is the origin Greek?" she asked.

"Yes," said the Pronouncer.

Her hand started tapping in regular rhythm. "P-a-l-y-n-o-l-o-g-i-c-a-l," she spelled slowly. "'Palynological.'"

There were cheers and whistles from the audience. Dylan rose from his chair, applauding, and even his father was clapping, but then he looked around self-consciously and quickly gripped his knees with his hands.

Ted Saunders turned to his co-host. "Now, Margaret, knowing the word was of Greek origin, did that help her?"

"I'm sure it did," she replied. "It told her that the 'i' sound in the middle was a 'y' rather than an 'i.'"

The Head Judge walked to the mike and adjusted it upward with his hand. "Ladies and gentlemen, we are down to the final two championship words. One—or both—of our finalists will walk away with the first-place trophy. I want to thank both spellers for providing us with the most exciting National Spelling Bee we've ever had." He motioned to Dylan to take the mike. "You're up," he said.

Dylan shot a nervous glance at his father before gripping the mike.

"The word is 'logorrhea,'" said the Pronouncer.

"Could I have a definition, please?"

"It means excessive talkativeness, especially when incoherent and uncontrollable."

Dylan took a deep breath. "'Logorrhea.' L-o-g-o-r-r-h-e-a." He stared hard at the Pronouncer.

"Congratulations!" said the Head Judge. "You have won the Scripps National Spelling Bee."

The crowd erupted in cheers and Mr. Watanabe did a little jig in front of his seat for joy. When the crowd quieted down, the Head Judge said, "Now, Dylan, let's see if you've got someone to share the prize money with."

He turned to Akeelah and, with a smile, gestured toward the mike.

"Bring it home," Dylan whispered to her.

"The word is 'pulchritude,'" the Pronouncer said.

Again Akeelah's remarkable memory came to her aid. She recalled Dr. Larabee in the school auditorium at the very first bee. She misspelled "pulchritude" and he corrected her, and of course she never forgot. But for a moment she seemed frozen in place. This was the final word, the word that could make her a national champion. She knew it cold, and yet she hesitated. She thought of all the people on whose shoulders she had ridden to this one special moment in time—her mother, Terrence, Derrick-T, the Crenshaw football team, Steve and the Korean grocer, and so many, many more.... She then said calmly, "'Pulchritude.' P-u-l-c-h-r-i-t-u-d-e."

The auditorium burst into thunderous applause. Dylan rushed up to the mike, took her hand, then put his arms around her and held her close. He whispered to her, "We've made history. It wouldn't be half as good if just one of us won."

Akeelah nodded her head. "Yeah, you're right. Well, congratulations, Dylan."

"Congratulations, Akeelah...."

They looked up at the ceiling simultaneously. Colored confetti was drifting down. Police sirens were blowing. Dylan and Akeelah accepted the trophy from the Head Judge and, with faces beaming, held it high above their heads. Dr. Larabee, Tanya, Georgia, Devon, and Mr. Welch made their way through the fans and photographers to join Akeelah onstage. Tanya threw her arms around her daughter and then gravely shook hands with Mr. Watanabe.

Akeelah managed to take Dr. Larabee aside.

"We did it," she said.

"No," he said, looking at her with absolute pride. "You did it."

She gave him a huge hug and then turned to Dylan. "Can I borrow the trophy for a minute?"

"Sure. It's half yours." He grinned. "We'll have to work out a custody arrangement."

Akeelah and Dr. Larabee held the victory trophy aloft as dozens of pictures were snapped of them in this victorious stance. She looked up at him and said, "The dream did come true, didn't it?"

"I always knew it would," he said. "I never had a single doubt."

The Present

Maybe the word I'm searchin' for is…what? Maybe it's 'magic.' Human magic….

My dreams did come true, and how many people's dreams ever come true? It was days before I came down from whatever cloud or star I was riding on high above the earth. Two days after Dylan and I won the National Bee, I turned twelve, we had a big birthday blowout—paid for by Mr. Watanabe!—and then we were back in South Los Angeles—Washington, D.C., a beautiful memory that I know will grow even more beautiful with time. And most of all, I will have it forever and ever.

The day after we returned, I was sitting at my computer puzzling over a starter chess program Dr. Larabee had bought me for my birthday when Mama knocked on my door. I told her to come in and she peeked around the opening holding a letter in her hand. It was wrinkled and coffee-stained.

"I want you to read this," she said.

"What is it?"

"A letter your daddy wrote me a few months before he was killed."

"I don't remember him ever going away long enough to write a letter."

Tanya smiled. "He didn't. We never went anywhere

183

without each other. But once in a while he'd have an urge to write me a letter. He said it was another way of communicating. Like the difference between TV and radio—that's how he put it. Writing the letter was the radio. More intimate. Over the years he must've written me a dozen or so. This was the last one he ever wrote. I've never shown it to anybody—or any of the letters—but I want you to read this one. After you read it, it belongs to you. I don't need it. I know it by heart."

She blew me a kiss good night and closed the door softly, leaving me alone with the letter. I sat at the computer and removed a lined sheet of paper from the envelope. He had filled both sides of the sheet.

Dear Tanya,

Sometimes I have a need to send words to you and through you to the children without seeing your face—or theirs. Words have always been my medium, just as kindness and caring mark you as the person you are. Charm is Devon's medium, charm and constant good will. Nurturing is Kiana's (how many dolls has she smothered to death with affection, leaving them in joyous rags?). Terrence's medium is heroism: he wants to pick up the sword and slay the evil dragon. And Akeelah? What is her medium? I would like to say "words," like me. But she has a far different relationship to words than I do. She dives into them, into their very architecture, and she's what—seven years old? How can that be? She is brilliant, Tanya, but I've never told her so because she does not need to know. She will discover this about herself soon enough (I hope not too soon), in her own time, and in

184

case I'm not here to guide her through the complex steps that will follow this recognition, I depend on you.

I have one important request to make. When Akeelah turns twelve, please buy her a paperback called *Three Negro Classics*. The classic of the three I want her to read is called *The Souls of Black Folk*, by W. E. B. DuBois. When she reads this book, she will understand why I asked her to; the layers of meaning will speak clearly to her. I will quote you only one passage to give you a sense of what lies in wait for her. You will find it on page 220. (I have made a few changes to clarify and update it.)

"The training of the schools we need today more than ever—the training of deft hands, quick eyes and ears and above all the broader, deeper, higher culture of gifted minds and pure hearts. The power of the ballot we need in sheer self-defense—else what shall save us from a second slavery? Freedom, too, the long-sought, we shall seek—the freedom of life and limb, the freedom to work and think, the freedom to love and aspire. Work, culture, liberty—all these we need, not singly but together, not successively but together, each growing and aiding each, and all striving toward that vaster ideal that swims before the Negro people, the ideal of human brotherhood, gained through the unifying ideal of Race; the ideal of fostering and developing the traits and talents of the Negro, not in opposition to or contempt for other races, but rather in large conformity to the greater ideals of the American Republic, in order that some day on American soil two world races may give each to each those characteristics both so sadly lack."

Akeelah will absorb the wisdom in this book, and my fervent wish is that, no matter what else she does with her life, she will add a chapter of her own to the unending struggle. That is my dream....

There was more, but when I got to the word "dream," I couldn't take in any more.

I looked at my father's photograph. I looked extra hard to see what he was saying to me. "So you were there, Daddy. You were in the auditorium and I know you were proud, but this is only the beginning, right? Is that what you're telling me? There are other places to go now, other things to do."

I don't have to wait for Mama to buy the book. I'll pick up a copy tomorrow at the library. There's no time like the present.

About the Writers

In 2000, **Doug Atchison** won the Nicholl Fellowship in Screenwriting for his screenplay of *Akeelah and the Bee*, which he later directed as a feature film for Lionsgate Films. He also co-wrote the screen version of Rebecca Gilman's award-winning play *Spinning into Butter*. He graduated from the University of Southern California's School of Cinema/Television and has taught directing and screenwriting at various universities.

James W. Ellison is the author of seven novels published by Doubleday, Little, Brown, and Dodd Mead, including the award-winning *I'm Owen Harrison Harding* and novelizations including *Finding Forrester, Two Brothers,* and *Rudy.* He lives in New York City with his wife Debra, son Owen, and daughter Brett.

You've read about Akeelah's amazing journey to the Scripps National Spelling Bee...

Now you too can organize your own spelling bee—here's how!

What you will need:

- Small, numbered sheets of paper

- Name tags for the contestants

- Paper, pad, and pens

- A bell

- A 2-minute timer

- A table and some chairs

- A dictionary

How to prepare your spelling bee:

✴ Set up a space for the bee by creating rows of chairs for the spellers, a small desk or table for the judges, and chairs for audience members (your parents and friends).

✴ Place numbered sheets of paper in a hat or a box and have each speller pull out a number. This determines the spelling order.

✴ Write each speller's name and number on a name tag. Spellers should then sit in numerical order facing the judges and the audience.

✴ Place a 2-minute timer, a little bell, and paper, pad, and pens on the judges' table.

✴ You will need two judges. Judge #1 will be responsible for reading the word and providing the language of origin and the definition. This judge will also write down the letters as the speller is spelling and check it against the correct spelling. Judge #2 is responsible for watching the 2-minute timer and informing spellers when time has run out.

Rules for your spelling bee:

* Each speller has 2 minutes to spell the word. If time runs out, the speller is disqualified.

* The speller should say the word, spell it, and then say the word again.

* The speller may stop mid-word and start from the beginning so long as no letters already spelled are changed.

* The judge may repeat the word multiple times to ensure the speller correctly understands the word.

* The speller may ask only 2 questions of the judge:

    1) Definition of the word, 2) Language of origin

* If the speller spells the word correctly, he or she sits back down. If the speller is incorrect, the judge rings the bell and the speller sits down with the audience.

* Once all spellers have had a turn, the next round begins with the remaining spellers until only two remain.

* The final two spellers will be given words until one misspells a word. The other speller is then given a chance to spell the same word. If he or she spells it right, the judge will supply a new word. If that word is spelled correctly, he or she wins!

(If the second word is spelled incorrectly, both spellers continue in the competition. The competition is over when one speller has correctly spelled the word that his or her opponent has misspelled, plus one additional word.)

Words for your spelling bee:

You can find words for your spelling bee in your dictionary. It will list the definition and pronunciation for each word. Here's a list of words to get you started:

Dissect	Pacifier	Averse
Personal	Pontificate	Pester
Brink	Notion	Pontoon
Traction	Underwrite	Aisle
Carnivore	Benign	Niece
Nostalgia	Stark	Corpse
Dire	Brocade	Sarcophagus
Autonomous	Pummel	Albumen
Bereft	Rebuff	Knack
Nuzzle	Scant	Condominium
Elite	Pseudonym	Initial
Autograph	Inactive	Therapy
Burnish	Collect	Catamaran
Beneficial	Alchemy	Homely

You can also download lists of words from the Scripps National Spelling Bee website:
http://www.spellingbee.com/studyaids.shtml

We hope you have fun organizing your spelling bee! Share your own story with us by sending an e-mail to publicity@newmarketpress.com and join our e-mail list to receive information on Newmarket Press books.

KR NEWMARKET MEDALLION EDITIONS FOR YOUNG READERS

*Media tie-in fiction and nonfiction in paperback editions
for middle-grade and young-adult readers*

Finding Forrester

A Novel by James W. Ellison
Based on the Screenplay Written by Mike Rich
The inspiring story of an unlikely friendship between a famous, reclusive novelist and an amazingly gifted teen who secretly yearns to be a writer. "Polished and compelling."—*The New York Times.* 192 pages. $9.95

Fly Away Home

A Novel by Patricia Hermes
Based on the Screenplay Written by Robert Rodat and Vince McKewin
This inspirational family adventure follows 14-year-old Amy and her inventor father as they attempt to teach geese how to fly. 160 pages. $7.95

Two Brothers: The Tale of Kumal and Sangha

A Novel by James W. Ellison
Based on the Screenplay Written by Alain Godard & Jean-Jacques Annaud
Inspired by the acclaimed family film from the maker of *The Bear*, a heart-warming nature tale about two tiger cubs born in the Southeast Asian jungle, who are separated from their parents and each other. 192 pages. $7.95

THREE CLASSIC WILDERNESS TALES BY JAMES OLIVER CURWOOD

The Bear

The movie *The Bear* was inspired by this exciting story originally titled *The Grizzly King.* Thor, a mighty grizzly, and Muskwa, a motherless bear cub, become companions in the Canadian wilderness. "As thrilling as the movie!"—*Kirkus Reviews.* 208 pages. $5.95

Baree: The Story of a Wolf-Dog

The thrilling story of a half-tame, half-wild wolf pup, who must grow up alone in the wilderness. "A timeless tale."—*ALA Booklist.* 256 pages. $5.95

Kazan: Father of Baree

Kazan struggles to survive the harsh Canadian wilderness, with his courageous mate, Gray Wolf. "Curwood has an invaluable gift of the born narrator."—*The New York Times Book Review.* 240 pages. $5.95

Newmarket Press books are available from your local bookseller or from Newmarket Press, Special Sales Department, 18 East 48th Street, New York, NY 10017; phone 212-832-3575 or 800-669-3903; fax 212-832-3629; email info@newmarketpress.com. Prices and availability are subject to change. Catalogs and information on quantity order discounts are available upon request. **www.newmarketpress.com**